THE NOBLE NEPHEW

Martha Kirkland

Zebra Books
Kensington Publishing Corp.
http://www.zebrabooks.com

ZEBRA BOOKS are published by

Kensington Publishing Corp.
850 Third Avenue
New York, NY 10022

Zebra and the Z logo Reg. U.S. Pat. & TM Off.

First Printing: August, 1998
10 9 8 7 6 5 4 3 2 1

Printed in the United States of America

TENDER TOUCH

Only after Duncan had drained the tankard and set the empty container back down on the table did Gemma notice that the cuff of his right sleeve was charred and that the skin on the underside of his wrist was red.

"Duncan!" she cried, catching hold of his hand. "You have burned yourself."

The gentleman was not certain which surprised him most, the fact that he was injured, or the fact that the lady had called him by his name. "So I have," he said, turning over his hand. "Do not be concerned. My man will take care of it."

"Please. I insist you allow me to put a soothing balm on it."

After assisting him to remove his coat, she turned the scorched cuffs of his shirtsleeves back from his wrists and forearms. Then she gently lifted both his hands and placed them in a bowl of warm water.

Without warning him what she was about to do, Miss Gemma Westin dipped her own hands into the water just long enough to wet them, then she took the soap and rubbed the cake between her palms until a rich lather formed. Her next action was almost Duncan's undoing, for to his total amazement, she lifted his right hand, and using her own soapy ones, she began to wash away the soot.

Duncan closed his eyes, not moving, not daring to breathe, while her hypnotic touch cast a spell upon him, introducing into his consciousness images he had no right to be contemplating—images of her trailing those marvelous fingers over other parts of his anatomy while he buried his face in the long, sun-kissed hair that tumbled about her shoulders . . .

Books by Martha Kirkland

THE GALLANT GAMBLER

THREE FOR BRIGHTON

THE NOBLE NEPHEW

Published by Zebra Books

*To our daughter, Lorraine Kirkland,
upon her graduation from UNCW.
Your dad and I are proud of you.*

Chapter One

"Adopt Ceddy? Never!" Gemma declared. Fear made the young lady's voice sound harsh, but at that moment she could no more control her emotions than she could fly across the broad marshy fens that were her home. "Never, I say. Not unless it be over my dead body!"

Miss Gemma Westin stared at the boy's mother, who stood in the doorway of the small, low-ceilinged bedchamber, a letter in her hand. "I vow to you, Nora, they shall not have him."

Mrs. Nora Creighton Westin returned her stepdaughter's look, her principal concern at that moment for the young lady whose sky-blue eyes were wide with anxiety. Nora knew well why Gemma was frightened, and why her English rose complexion had gone ashen, emphasizing the sprinkle of freckles across her pretty nose. Gemma had lost her father just over a year ago, and Nora and Ceddy, though not related to her by blood, were the only family she had left in the world. Without them, she would be all alone.

"I am shocked at you, Nora. How can you consider such an action for even an instant?"

"I have not had an opportunity to consider it," Nora replied, the slight tremor in her usually calm voice betraying her own qualms. "The proposition is as much a surprise to me as it is to you."

"Was there anything in Lady Montgomery's first letter to indicate that they had such a scheme in mind? Anything to make you suspect that they wanted to adopt Ceddy?"

"Of course not. Had there been, I would have told you." She scanned the first sheet of the letter that had only just arrived. "Here, let me read you what Lady Montgomery has written, for she and Sir Frederick agree that—"

"I do not care what Lady Montgomery has written! We have not come to such a pass that our only alternative is to hand Ceddy over to strangers."

Tossing her quill down in anger, Gemma pushed away from the handsome rosewood desk. The desk had belonged to her mother, and it was the only piece of furniture Gemma had brought with her when she, Nora, and Ceddy had removed from Howarth Manor to the Cottage. To Gemma's discomfort, Nora cast a meaningful look at the marbleboard copybook that served as their accounts ledger. The several sheets of vellum that had been crumpled and cast aside, strewn between the ledger and the pewter inkstand, gave evidence of Gemma's continuing struggle with their finances.

"I know, I know," she said, "you need say nothing." Honesty demanded that Gemma acknowledge the truth, that their financial situation was, to say the least, precarious. She and Nora had outrun their funds again, with a full three weeks to be got through before the midsummer quarter day.

In the thirteen months since the untimely demise of Philip Westin, running out of funds had become a disturbingly common occurrence for the gentleman's daughter and his young widow. Because Gemma had no money of her own, and Nora's portion was but three hundred pounds per annum, making ends meet was proving more difficult than either lady had imagined.

Knowing herself to be a drain on Nora's already strained finances, Gemma lamented the fact that she could not touch her inheritance for another eight years. "If only I were thirty," she said.

Nora shook her head, causing a curl to come loose from the knot that never seemed to subdue her dark-blond tresses for more than a few minutes at a time. "Do not wish those years away," she said, shoving the curl behind her ear. "Time passes all too quickly as it is. I know, for I find it difficult to credit that my next birthday will find me a woman of thirty-four."

"But if I were thirty, I could have my inheritance, and we need not be obliged to pinch every penny just to keep body and soul together. Of what good is three thousand pounds if we starve to death before I am old enough to take possession of it?"

"We are in no danger of starving, my love. As long as your cousin continues to manage the estate in a conscientious manner, my widow's portion is assured. Further, Howarth Cottage is mine for my lifetime, so we cannot be put out. Unfortunately, there is more to be considered than food and lodging."

"I know you are concerned for Ceddy's future, Nora, but—"

"I am more than concerned. I am beside myself with worry, for I do not know what will become of my son."

Nora trod across the colorful rag rug that all but covered the polished oak floor of the small room, then she sat upon the edge of Gemma's half tester bed. "Ceddy cannot continue to study with the curate. The lad is intelligent beyond his eleven years, and he is fast outstripping the worthy Mr. Newley's abilities as an instructor.''

In hopes of preventing any further reference to that ''worthy'' gentleman who had begun of late to pay special attention to her, Gemma hurried to agree that Master Cedric Creighton should be at Eton. ''It is what his father and my father would have wanted.''

''Of course they would. Unfortunately, neither of my husbands left me with sufficient funds to send Ceddy to Eton, or even some less prestigious school.''

Nora's cheeks grew pink at the vehemence of her last statement. ''Do not misunderstand me, my love, I do not fault either gentlemen—I assure you I do not—for how could they know they would not be here to see to the matter themselves? Still, the sad fact is they are not here, and it is left to you and me to do the best we can with our lives and with Ceddy's. And I need not tell you that without a proper education there is little chance of my son entering into a suitable profession.''

No, Nora need not tell her. Like the boy's mother, Gemma was aware of the effect their straitened circumstances would have on Ceddy's future. ''We will just have to be more frugal.''

''But we are being as prudent as possible, and there is little else left on which we may economize.''

Gemma looked about her as if hoping a solution might present itself. Unfortunately, all she spied was the bright new pink-and-white striped pasteboard hatbox that sat atop the chiffonnier. ''I will return the three new bonnets I had from Madame Yvette's,'' she said. ''I have not worn them, so they may be resold—''

''No! Your unselfishness does you credit, my love, but we could never be frugal enough to save two hundred pounds per annum for school fees. Besides, you deserve to have a few pretty things. You are a young woman, and you have been in mourning far too long. It is time you had some new bonnets to show off those lovely blue eyes and your sun-kissed hair."

"And my sun-kissed nose?" Gemma added, wrinkling that member, which was the bane of her existence.

"That, too," Nora said, smiling for the first time since she came upstairs, "for without the freckles, you would not be our Gemma."

With a sigh of resignation, Gemma reached her hand out for the letter. "May I read for myself what Lady Montgomery has to say?"

"Of course. As you will see, Sir Frederick still wants to meet Ceddy before coming to any decision. Though if I had suspected that he wished to adopt my son before naming him heir to Montgomery Park, I would have refused the offer when the first letter came."

"Certainly you would have," Gemma agreed, reassured by her stepmother's words, "for even if Sir Frederick's wealth should prove to be a fortune, Ceddy is not for sale."

Gemma scanned the two sheets. "It says here that Sir Frederick means to bring his nephew along to advise him upon the legalities." She looked up from the pages. "If he has a nephew, why does he not name that gentleman his heir? Surely a nephew has more claim upon him than Ceddy, who is but a great-nephew. And his wife's great-nephew at that."

"Actually," Nora said, "Sir Frederick has two nephews, one of whom bears the Montgomery name. I never met either gentleman, but I remember that Ceddy's father was not fond of one of them. Which one, I cannot recall."

"Let us hope it is not the one who is on his way here, for according to the letter, Sir Frederick and Lady Montgomery mean to wait upon us quite soon. 'If it will not inconvenience you,' " Gemma read aloud, " 'we will arrive at Duddingham some time in the early afternoon of June first. At which time we will—' " She stopped. "June first? But that is—"

"Today," Nora replied with a touch of asperity. "Notice the date of the letter."

Gemma did as she was bid. "This letter was dated a full two weeks ago. What could have delayed it for so long?"

"What indeed?"

At Nora's uncharacteristically derisive tone, Gemma said, "Did Amos forget to ask at the inn if anything had come for Howarth Cottage?"

Nora shook her head. "You know he did not."

"Then what—"

"The letter was picked up with the post for Howarth Manor more than a sennight ago, and Alicia has only just this hour seen fit to send it down to the cottage."

"Unread?"

When Nora chose not to dignify the question with an answer, the two women exchanged knowing looks. "The wafer was broken," Nora continued, "but Alicia claims she misread the direction."

"An honest mistake," Gemma said, her voice dripping with sarcasm. "Mrs. *Philip* Westin being so easily misread for Mrs. *Titus* Westin, especially when the name is written in such neat copperplate."

"As you say, my love. But let us put the incident from our minds, for I fear we shall be obliged to be much in Alicia's company in the coming days. She and your Cousin Titus have invited Sir Frederick and Lady Montgomery to be their guests at Howarth Manor."

"Titus is all goodness," Gemma said dryly. "I suppose it is too much to hope that he will not make a complete toady of himself in Sir Frederick's presence. As for Alicia, I pray she does not display that lack of reserve she—"

"Shh, my love." Nora looked toward the door to assure herself they had not been overheard. "I see you are still angry with Titus and Alicia on my account, but I wish you would let it be. I did not expect them to invite me to remain at the manor, and even had they done so, I would have refused.''

"But it was your home.''

Nora rose and walked over to the window that offered a view of the small wildflower garden below. "Surely you remember how it felt to be usurped as mistress of the establishment. After all, you were sixteen years old when your father married me, and you were quite used to ordering things as you liked them.''

"Goose,'' Gemma said, "that was different. How could I not welcome you as the new mistress, when Papa was so delighted with his pretty new bride. Besides, you were the big sister I had always wanted, and Ceddy was the little brother I thought never to have. I believe I loved you both instantly.''

Having revealed so much, Gemma fell silent, not wanting Nora to hear the emotion she could not hide. She had been unbearably lonely before Nora and Ceddy came to Howarth Manor. Though she had adored her father, Philip Westin had no idea how to care for a motherless daughter, so for seven years he had left her under the supervision of a governess who, though an excellent teacher, was formal to a fault and as unapproachable as she was strict.

When Nora and Ceddy arrived, they were like gifts from heaven to the lonely sixteen-year-old. They were two blond-haired, gray-eyed rays of sunshine who spread their warmth to include Gemma, and for the next five years she basked in that warmth, happier than she had ever been. Now, with her father gone, Gemma was an orphan, alone in the world save for the two people whose only ties to her were those of the heart, and she could not—would not—let anyone take them from her. No matter what she had to do, she would not let the Montgomerys adopt Ceddy and take him away.

"Have you seen Ceddy?" Nora asked, interrupting Gemma's thoughts. "I must find him before his aunt and uncle arrive, for who can say how much grime may have found its way to his face and hands."

"The last time I saw him, he was down at the lane, sitting on a limb of the service tree, picking the berries and putting them in that disreputable pouch he carries. One may venture a guess as to the nefarious purpose for which the berries are intended."

"Ammunition against the smithy's two rascally sons," Nora replied with a certain resignation. She looked beyond the flower-filled garden, her gaze following the moss-stained flagstone walk that led from the cottage door to the lane. At the edge of the lane, a mounting block stood quite near the base of an ancient service tree fully seventy feet tall—a tree whose sturdy limbs and shiny, deep green leaves offered a degree of privacy to a lad who had not yet grown accustomed to living in a much smaller house. Unfortunately, the sturdy limbs held no lads at the moment.

Sighing, Nora said, "Well, he is not there now, and a groat will net you a shilling he is at the river even as we speak."

Gemma smiled to hear her father's favorite phrase on Nora's lips. "Let us *hope* the scamp is at the river, for rowing his boat or fishing from the weir would leave him merely dirty. Must I remind you that there is always the windmill?"

"Do not say so!" Nora closed her eyes as if to deny the picture of her son at the fen, knee deep in watery reeds and sedge. "He must be brought home without delay, for what sort of impression will he make if he is covered in brackish mud?"

Gemma did not give voice to her true thoughts, which

were a hope that the older couple would take Ceddy in instant dislike. Instead, she said, "I daresay Lady Montgomery is aware of the less endearing habits of eleven-year-old boys. After all, she had the raising of her grandson.' "

While the Westin ladies changed their costumes prior to searching for the missing boy, an elegant maroon chaise and four, tastefully picked out in gold, entered the quiet village of Duddingham. Unaccustomed to witnessing such elegance, many a passerby stopped to gawk at the conveyance, the maroon-and-gold liveried coachman, and the two outriders.

"A handsome village," Sir Frederick remarked, leaning away from the tufted satin squabs to look out the window of the coach. "Rather more prosperous looking than I had expected."

"And so colorful," Lady Montgomery added, gazing at the two-story thatched cottages and shops that lined the village high street. Most of the edifices were covered in stucco, then painted pink or gray, and at the sight, her ladyship's soft brown eyes showed a hint of disappointment. "Where are the picturesque Norman cottages I had expected to see? Are there none left standing?"

The tall, slender gentleman who sat with his back to the horses chose to answer the lady's question. "The prosperity of the Tudor and Georgian years enabled the villagers to replace their humbler abodes. Though I am persuaded, ma'am," he added with a wink in Sir Frederick's direction, "that had they known you would be dissatisfied with the new cottages, they would have kept the cramped and molding old flint and mortar ones, never mind the inconvenience to themselves and to their families."

A smile softened Sir Frederick's craggy face. "I vow, Duncan, 'tis such jokesters as you who give barristers a bad name." He patted his wife's mittened hand. "How shall we make him pay for such impudence, my dear?"

"Find him a wife," the lady replied. "That should take care of him nicely."

Sir Frederick chuckled. "A capital idea. And because my nephew fancies a future in politics, I recommend a very *young* lady. One with a tendency to giggle."

"And one who eschews books of all kinds," her ladyship suggested. "A gel whose every waking thought is concentrated upon the cut of her clothes and which of her cicisbeo she will allow to escort her to the next al fresco breakfast."

When the prospective bridegroom shuddered like a spaniel just come from the water, the older couple laughed. "I am persuaded you have his measure, my dear," Sir Frederick said. "When next we are in town, you must look out just such a young lady. The sillier the better."

"I pray you, Aunt Evelyn, if you have any regard for me, do no such thing."

Since Duncan was able at that moment to point out a beautiful old Norman church, whose walled church yard boasted one of the ancient round towers for which East Anglia was noted, the subject of young ladies was dropped, and he was allowed to enjoy his bachelor status in peace.

Mr. Duncan Jamison knew he would one day be obliged to wed, for an intelligent, well-connected hostess was essential to a man with political ambitions, but he was in no hurry to tie himself to one female. Furthermore, time and circumstances were on his side. Because he was a successful barrister, and next in line to a baronetcy and a well-run estate that would supplement his income by about five thousand pounds per annum, the gentleman was considered a very desirable *parti* by the ton and by the matchmaking mamas.

His desirability notwithstanding, Duncan had only just celebrated his thirtieth birthday. With a number of years still left on his plate, he felt he had plenty of time at his disposal and might with a free conscience delay the inevitable leg shackling. As well, though he had been pursued by many a pretty young lady, he had not met even one who possessed that certain something in her style that would inspire him to tie himself to her for life.

When it came to alliances of a less permanent kind, Duncan had taken a page from the book of his rather picturesque valet, whose conquests were legendary throughout the pubs of London. "When choosing a likely lass to warm me bed of an evening," the valet boasted, "I be certain she's got no plans for the church porch come morning."

It had seemed good advice, and so far Duncan had followed it to the letter.

As for Mr. Jamison's heart, that organ remained whole and intact, its sole function to pump blood throughout his lean, athletic body. He had decided long ago that love was just a word poets grew maudlin about; in the real world, it did not exist. Except, of course, for the attachment existing between Sir Frederick and Lady Montgomery.

Forty-five years those two had been wed, and only genuine affection could have sustained them through the tragedies of the last twenty years. Having lost their only daughter and her husband in a carriage accident, they had taken their grandson into their home. They had doted on the youngster, unable to deny him anything, and when he had joined the Royal Navy, and been so fortunate as to serve aboard the *Victory* with Nelson, they had been as happy for him as he was for himself. When tragedy struck again at the battle of Trafalgar, and their grandson was killed, the Montgomerys were practically inconsolable.

It was their very real grief that had prompted Duncan to encourage them in this plan involving Master Cedric Creighton, the young son of Evelyn Montgomery's deceased nephew. Of course, Sir Frederick had two nephews of his own—Duncan was one of them and his cousin, Nevil Montgomery, the other. Unfortunately, they were both grown men. What the elderly couple needed was a youngster—someone they could watch grow into manhood, someone they could nurture and love and who would love them in return.

They needed solace—the kind only an innocent child could give them—and Duncan doubted that Nevil even knew the meaning of the word.

The son of Sir Frederick's younger brother, Nevil Montgomery was arguably the next in line to be heir to his uncle's estate and fortune, but in his twenty-nine years, Nevil had shown interest in nothing but gaming and riotous living. If he had ever committed an unselfish act, it had gone undetected by his family and cohorts alike.

As for Duncan, the son of Sir Frederick's sister, he was inordinately fond of his uncle and aunt, but he had plans of his own, and as his father's only son, he had no need of his uncle's money. Therefore, he saw no reason why his uncle should not make the Creighton boy his heir. That is, if the lad proved likable.

"It should not be long now," he said after the carriage passed through the village then bumped across a handsome old stone bridge arched above the waters of the gently flowing Nene—waters that reflected the cloudless blue of the sky.

The trip had been easy, with the roads neither so dry the horses raised clouds of choking dust, or so damp the earth was turned into a quagmire, and while the coachman cracked his whip in the air, urging the team on, the occupants of the coach grew silent, watchful. With four reasonably fresh horses in harness, they needed little more than a quarter hour to cover the three miles from the village to the Westin estate.

When the driver halted the team in the lane opposite a pleasant two-story cottage whose front garden displayed a riot of wildflowers bordered by thick rows of heartsease— their velvety yellow-and-purple faces opening to the warmth of the late-spring sun—the Montgomerys clasped hands for a moment, exchanging nervous glances.

"We are here," her ladyship whispered, her eyes suddenly damp.

"Yes, my dear," her husband replied, his voice suspiciously husky. "We are here at last."

They would not stay long, of course, for Duncan's aunt had received a letter from Mrs. Titus Westin, the new mistress of Howarth Manor, inviting the travelers to treat the manor as their home while they were in Suffolk. Though they had accepted the invitation, it had been decided earlier in the day that they would stop first at the cottage for a brief exchange of greetings with Mrs. Philip Westin.

Not that Duncan was deceived for an instant by this supposed show of civility. The couple stopped at the cottage for one reason, and one only: They were eager for a look at the boy they had not seen since his mother remarried and moved to Duddingham, eager to know if the lad would suit them and they him.

"Carriage be in the lane, mistress," Amos Littlejohn yelled from the bottom of the narrow staircase. At his call, the Westin ladies rushed from their respective bedchambers, Nora busily tying the pale-green ribbons of a most fetching lace cap, and Gemma straightening the embroidered lawn fichu she had added to her new primrose muslin frock.

"Oh, dear," Nora said, "it is the Montgomerys, and we have not even begun to search for Ceddy." Leaning over the banister, she called down to their man of all work, who was already halfway down the short corridor leading to the kitchen and still room, "Amos, wait, please. I have need of you."

Amos Littlejohn peeped from around the stairwell wall, his unfortunate orange hair protruding from his head in all directions like sprigs of hay from a newly piled rick. "Yes, mistress," he replied.

The homely giant, along with two housemaids, had accompanied the Westin ladies when they removed from Howarth Manor to the cottage. Somewhat older than Gemma's twenty-two years, Amos was a bit simple, and for that reason Alicia was afraid of him, refusing to keep him on at the manor, even in his capacity as the gardener's assistant.

Born on the estate, Amos would have been lost if required to move too far away, so Nora had insisted he come with them to the cottage; as she had put it, as protector for a house full of women. It was a decision she had not regretted, for other than being amazingly strong and seemingly tireless, Amos possessed a native intuitiveness that more than made up for any mental deficiency. Not only was he an accurate weather prognosticator, but he was also adept at finding lost items.

Nora wasted no time in bidding him to find Ceddy. "He could be any one of a number of places. But wherever he may be, tell him he must come home on the instant, for his aunt and uncle have arrived."

Amos bobbed his head several times. "I'll find him, mistress. Not to worry, I'll bring him home."

"Thank you, Amos. I knew I could count on you."

"Wait," Gemma said, "show the visitors in first, Amos, then while you go to the windmill to see if Ceddy is there, I will search for him at the river."

The servant paused only a moment, then he pulled his forelock respectfully. "Yes, miss."

The ladies waited only until Amos had shown the guests to the larger and more formal of the three small rooms on the ground floor, then they tiptoed down the stairs that ended just a few feet from the front entrance.

"I will return as soon as I find Ceddy," Gemma said, keeping her voice low.

"Traitor!" Nora replied. "Do not think I do not see the design behind your scheme, for you mean to leave me to face Sir Frederick and Lady Montgomery alone."

"Goose. You have only to stand firm."

"Easy for you to say, especially if you are safely at the river while I assert myself. You know how abhorrent I find it to cause someone distress, and the Montgomerys have always been so kind to Ceddy. Never once have they failed to remember him with some gift on his birthday. This last year, they sent him a golden guinea to do with as he wished."

Gemma mumbled a most unladylike word. "Do they think the boy is for sale for a guinea and a few trinkets? If they offered you ten *thousand* guineas, it would not be enough. Now go into the drawing room, there's a good girl, and tell them so in no uncertain terms."

Having said her piece, Gemma hurried outside and down the flagstone walk, never once looking in the direction of the rose arbor just to the right of the door where Mr. Duncan Jamison sat.

"So," the gentleman said once the young lady in yellow was out of hearing, "they want money for the lad. And a fortune at that!"

From what his uncle and aunt had told him, Duncan had not expected the mother to be mercenary, but it would appear that she was allowing herself to be influenced by this other person. Of course, if finances were their primary motive, it would make the adoption go that much smoother. In his experience, legalities were got through more easily when only money was involved and not the heart.

"But," he said aloud, "they must give over on such an exorbitant price."

Ten thousand pounds. Absurd! Furthermore, once the money changed hands, Duncan meant to see to it personally that all ties between the boy and those two avaricious women were severed. "If I have anything to do with the matter, neither the mother nor her scheming advisor will ever come near Ceddy Creighton again."

Chapter Two

Duncan had remained outside the cottage, taking a seat on a small wrought-iron bench beneath the fragrant rose arbor, to allow his aunt and uncle a few moments of privacy for their reunion with the boy and his mother. It had been his intention to join the older couple directly, but now he decided he would do better to follow the young lady in yellow. Whoever she was—Miss Westin, he presumed— she had said she was going in search of the lad, and if that was so, Duncan wanted to see Master Ceddy for himself and hear what the schemer said to the boy.

His only motive his wish to protect his aunt and uncle, Duncan waited until the young woman traversed the flag-stone path and crossed the lane, then he left the seclusion of the arbor and followed her. She was inadequately dressed for the out-of-doors, not having stopped to fetch a bonnet or to change her kid slippers for walking boots, yet she moved quickly, as though familiar with the terrain, and Duncan was obliged to step lively so as not to lose her when she hurried around a section of uncleared scrub.

It was strange country, the fens, a flat land with enormous skies, yet it had a haunting beauty all its own. Once a vast swamp that covered most of East Anglia, the fens had been drained by the large landowners to make way for farmland, and few uncultivated areas remained. However, this large stretch of land opposite the cottage was not under cultivation, and when Duncan saw the patch of uncleared scrub ahead, he knew its purpose: It was game cover, and this area had been left for the enjoyment of the hunter.

Knowing a moment's trepidation, Duncan hoped he would not find his attempt at detective work rewarded by a bullet to the back. He was as inappropriately dressed as the young lady, having chosen that morning to wear a bottle-green coat and fawn breeches, and it occurred to him, that dressed in those particular colors, he might easily be mistaken for prey and shot by some overzealous sportsman.

Fortunately, the scrub was not extensive, and after he rounded it, Duncan found that very little obscured his view save a couple of scraggly goat willows whose white catkins had not yet blown away. Pausing beside the small trees, he watched the young woman as she traversed a quarter mile of springy ground, ground that sloped downward slightly as it led to the banks of what he supposed must be a tributary of the Nene River.

While Duncan stood partially concealed by the willows, the young woman stepped to the edge of a small, weathered dock, where she called the boy's name. "Ceddy! Ceddy! If you hear me, please come in."

Receiving no answer, she turned and hurried upstream toward a dilapidated weir. Duncan followed. The noise of the river spilling through the wooden slats of the weir covered the sounds of his approach, but when the girl stopped suddenly, he was obliged to stop as well, taking refuge only a few feet away behind a tall, thick hawthorn bush.

While he waited to see what she would do next, a breeze filled with the aroma of moist earth and decaying vegetation blew at her skirts, molding the thin muslin to her long and rather shapely legs and exposing a pair of well-turned ankles. As susceptible as the next man to the sight of a comely figure, Duncan studied her unabashedly.

She was a pretty enough female, if one admired the fresh, country look. Of medium height, she was about twenty-one or -two, and though Duncan could detect no engagement ring upon her finger, he could not imagine that the local lads had failed to notice the way her honey-blond hair shone like gold in the afternoon sun, or that her eyes were the pure blue of a cloudless sky.

Of course, there were those freckles! Sprinkled across a decidedly pert nose, they were far from dignified; still, they seemed to suit her face, and Duncan could not totally despise them.

She moved closer to the weir, and it appeared that she meant to climb aboard the rickety wooden structure. Since its main purpose was to dam up the gently moving water, thereby forming a pool whose depth was at least six feet, Duncan debated the advisability of allowing her to test the weir's strength.

Before he could think how to stop her without surprising her into pitching forward into the water, she totally disarmed him. While he watched, his mouth agape, she bent down, caught the hem of her primrose frock in either hand, then stood and lifted both skirt and petticoats, draping them over her shoulders as though they were a cape.

Duncan could not believe his eyes, for with her skirts up, her knee-length drawers were in full view, and though she revealed a goodly portion of her shapely legs, it was her shapely derriere that claimed his attention. The drawers were not overly snug, but the young lady had obviously begun to perspire from her speedy jaunt from the cottage to the weir, and the moisture made the thin lawn adhere provocatively to her rounded bottom.

Though hers was not the first female posterior Duncan had been pleased to observe, it was certainly the first he had ever been privy to outside a lady's boudoir. The unexpectedness of the view, enhanced as it was by the bright sunshine, caused a suggestion of moisture to form inside his suddenly snug neckcloth. While he reached up to tug the constricting cravat away from his Adam's apple, the young woman stepped up onto the weir.

After shading her eyes with her hand, she called the boy's name again. She must have spotted him, for she began to wave her arm above her head, motioning him to come to her.

Certain she would fall into the water at any moment, Duncan stepped from behind the willow. "Hey, there!" he called. "Watch what you are about! Unless you are resolved to tumble headfirst into the water, I would advise you to move back onto the shore."

Tumbling into the water had been the furthest thing from Gemma's mind, but at the unexpected sound of a man's voice, she very nearly did just that. Startled that she was not alone, she turned quickly, and at sight of the tall stranger, she spoke without thinking. "What the devil are you doing there? Spying on me?"

"Definitely," he replied, a touch of amusement in his voice. He let his gaze travel her length. "In fact, I may take up spying as a hobby, for until two minutes ago, I had no idea it paid off in such, shall we say, unexpected ways."

Only just remembering that she had lifted her skirt to protect the muslin from being snagged by the splintered wood of the weir, Gemma hastily pushed the material from her shoulders, smoothing it into place once it fell to her ankles.

Her face had grown decidedly warm, and to her further embarrassment, the stranger had the audacity to chuckle at her actions. "A bit late for that," he said.

The man's mocking grin produced just the hint of a dimple in his left cheek, and though he was easily the handsomest man Gemma had ever seen, with eyes as green as the leaf of a dog rose, she knew a strong desire to see him floating facedown in the clear water of the pool below.

"I asked what you were doing here. This happens to be private land, and you are definitely trespassing."

"Possibly," he said, strolling toward her as though he cared not a fig that he trespassed, "but I doubt the land belongs to you, either. Therefore, I should imagine I have as much right to be here as you do."

"My father had this weir built," she said, as though that proved her claim.

When the man made no comment, Gemma added, "The tributary is normally only a few feet deep, and Papa wanted to raise the water level to improve the fishing."

"Is that what you were doing?" he asked, a look of devilment in his eyes. "Fishing?"

"Sir!"

"I cannot say I have ever seen it done in just that manner, but having been the recipient of a most interesting view, I should be the last person to cast aspersions on any new methods of—"

"A gentleman would have looked away."

He raised one rather sardonic eyebrow. "You believe that, do you?"

Feeling herself at a decided disadvantage, Gemma took a step toward the bank, her intention to jump free of the weir and exit the area with all speed and as much dignity as possible. Unfortunately, the moment she moved, she felt a tug at her skirt, a tug that told her plainly her fears had been realized; the muslin had been soundly caught by one of the splintered boards.

Not wanting to tear the first new dress she had worn in more than a year, she stopped immediately and turned to see how to free herself. To her dismay, freedom was impossible; only a contortionist could have reached the imprisoning board without putting enough stress on the fabric to rip it.

"May I be of service?" the man asked, his lips twitching as though he was on the verge of laughing again.

Because he made not the least effort to hide his amusement, Gemma was tempted to give him the set down he so richly deserved, then send him on his way. And she would have done so had she been able to save both her pride and her new frock.

The frock won out.

Resigned to her fate, she stood perfectly still, her hands at her sides while the man came closer. He stopped not two feet away from her, and with an exaggerated sweep of his arm, he lifted his curly-brimmed beaver, revealing light-brown hair cut rather short. "Shall I?" he asked, making her a bow that was as mocking as the light in his eyes.

This close, those eyes were a lighter green than Gemma had thought, with little flecks of gold near the centers, and as she watched, their expression changed. They seemed to be taking her measure—not male to female, as they had done earlier, but person to person—and Gemma had the lowering thought that they were not pleased with what they saw. All signs of humor had left his lean, sculptured face, and not even the symmetry of his well-formed lips could soften the uncompromisingly square chin.

Without touching her, he reached around behind her and carefully extricated the muslin. He did not let go of the material immediately as she had expected, but brought it forward so he could remove the sliver of wood.

"There," he said, dropping the splinter to the ground and moving aside, "you are free to continue upon your chosen path, with nothing to hinder you or do you harm." He pinned her with those measuring eyes. "I wonder, madam, could you be persuaded to extend the same courtesy to those you meet along the way?"

Not sure what he meant by such an enigmatic remark, and unsure what she should answer, Gemma chose the safest course, falling back upon common civility. "How do you do," she said. "I am Gemma Westin. I live just across the lane at Howarth Cottage."

He took the hand she offered, bowing over her fingers. "Your servant, Miss Westin."

It mattered not at all that he had failed to tell her his name, for Gemma was too bemused to hear anything other than the wild beating of her own heart. At the touch of his hand, she had received a shock not unlike that of the electricity demonstration she and Ceddy had participated in the previous month at the country fair.

Always eager to try something new, Ceddy had paid the sum of one pence to a cheap-jack who cranked up a little black box, then touched a metal wand to the boy's finger. The current had made Ceddy's hair stand on end. Not content with his own experience, the boy had insisted that Gemma pay her pence as well. She had agreed, and the resulting shock had done more than make her hair stand on end; it had surged from her finger all the way up her arm, causing her to squeal and snatch her hand away while the crowd of onlookers laughed.

When the tall stranger had taken her hand in his just then, she had felt again that current of electricity, though this time no one was laughing. Especially not Gemma Westin.

"I am Duncan Jamison," he said at last, releasing her fingers. "I have accompanied Sir Frederick and Lady Montgomery to Suffolk, and I feel it only fair to warn you that I will not let you, or anyone else, hurt them. Furthermore," he added, "should you be entertaining thoughts of unlimited access to their purse for the next dozen years, dipping into it whenever you are pressed for funds, allow me to disabuse you of that notion. Once this adoption is settled, and the monies agreed upon are paid, I expect you to disappear from Ceddy's life forever. No letters. No visits. And no chicanery."

Too stunned to reply, Gemma stared at Mr. Duncan Jamison, noting the uncompromising set of his jaw. His handsome face was masked by the aloof, unreadable mien of the experienced barrister, and Gemma had the unpleasant feeling that she was under suspicion for some crime. More than suspected; already charged, tried, and found guilty.

"Chicanery?" she repeated, anger helping her find her voice. "You would know more about that subject than I."

"I?"

"You, sir. As a barrister, you must deal with it all the time. Although," she continued, "as an officer of the court, surely you are obliged, at least some of the time, to take note of the facts. Fact one: I did not seek out the Montgomerys or their purse. Fact two: I did not petition them to come here. They came to Suffolk without invitation, their design to take Ceddy from his home."

Gemma paused for breath, and though she was rigid with anger, she was also frightened, for Sir Frederick had wealth and power at his disposal, and the man who stood before her appeared a more than formidable opponent. Still, she would not give Ceddy up without a fight.

"If, perchance, a few other facts have escaped your

notice, Mr. Jamison, allow me to call your attention to one particularly pertinent detail.''

"And that would be?''

"Ceddy is not an orphan. He has a family. He has his mother and he has me, and neither of us is willing to surrender him for adoption.''

Duncan was about to inform her that he knew her last statement to be a whisker, for he had heard her instructions to Mrs. Nora Westin, bidding the mother accept no less than ten thousand pounds for her son. As luck would have it, however, at that very moment the lad himself drew near, paddling upstream in a small punt. The narrow, flat-bottomed boat had a pole lashed to its side, its purpose for maneuvering in the shallower water downstream, but it had also been equipped with oars for the deeper water near the weir, and though the lad was small for his age, he handled the oars with competence.

"Perhaps,'' Duncan said quietly, looking from the woman to the boy in the boat, "we should leave this discussion for later.''

Before she could answer, Ceddy called out to her. "Are you all right, Gemma?'' he asked, his gray eyes shooting figurative arrows at Duncan.

"Miss Westin is just fine,'' Duncan replied, "I merely saw her standing on the weir and was afraid she might fall into the pool.''

He smiled then, employing a theatrical trick he often used in court, one that invited the onlookers to enjoy a joke at his expense. "You may call me a fop if you like, but I just had this coat from my tailor in London, and I had no wish to ruin it by diving into the water to save the young lady should she fall.''

Master Cedric Creighton was obviously not impressed by the barrister's theatrics. Pushing a dark-blond lock of hair back from his forehead with a far from clean hand, he continued to scowl at Duncan. "If you had jumped in after Gemma," he said, "you would have spoiled your fancy coat for no reason. My sister is the best swimmer in the whole of East Anglia. It was her taught me how, just like she taught me how to pole and paddle this punt."

"But not to fish," the young lady added, giving the lad a stern look that clearly said, "mind your manners."

The boy received the message and averted his gaze to the oar he was obliged to continue dipping into the water to avoid drifting back downstream. "Gemma does not like to fish," the boy added, his tone, if not his manner, less hostile.

"You know it is the bait I dislike," the young lady replied with a shiver. "Worms and bugs. Revolting!"

At this, the boy smiled, revealing a gap in his top teeth where a permanent molar still had not grown in to replace a lost infant tooth. It was a disarming smile, boyish and spontaneous, and after witnessing it, Duncan was forced to acknowledge that Ceddy and Miss Westin shared a sort of camaraderie.

The lad had called her his sister, yet they were not related. Theirs was a connection only, and a few minutes ago, Duncan would have sworn that the woman had no affection for the boy. Now, however, he was beginning to wonder if his original estimate of her sentiments might have been a bit hasty. If nothing else, she did not wish young Ceddy to be upset by this unexpected meeting.

Since that was his objective as well, Duncan bowed to Miss Westin. "Your pardon, madam, if I maligned you, but until today, I had never met a lady who numbered swimming and boating among her accomplishments."

She gave him a look that said she knew full well that his apology did not include his earlier accusation of chicanery. "I am aware that most ladies cannot swim, but I am not most ladies. My governess thought it a lesson as necessary to my education as French and geography.''

"A most unusual curriculum," Duncan observed.

"True, but my governess was a woman of strong opinions, and she believed it important for anyone who lived *near* the water to know how to survive *in* the water. She would not tolerate my ignorance of the skill and applied herself to the task of teaching me, for she deemed the inability to swim to be a death warrant just waiting to be delivered. With that, at least, I agreed with her, for one never knows when the water will suddenly reach up and pull one in.''

She looked directly into Duncan's eyes, and there was no mistaking her purpose. "For someone who cannot swim, falling into the water is not unlike the plight of a poor widow who finds that her most prized possession is coveted by a rich man. Like the hapless person in the water, the widow has but one choice, to sink or swim. She must pit her strength against the rich man and his might, and though it prove a struggle, she dare not give in.''

While Duncan had followed Gemma from the cottage, Nora had entered the parlor to the left of the vestibule to greet her first husband's aunt and uncle. She had not seen them in more than a half dozen years, and the changes time and bereavement had wrought in them were more than she had expected.

Sir Frederick stood beside the empty fireplace, giving cursory glances at one or two of the porcelain figurines arranged on the carved oak mantelpiece, while Lady Montgomery sat across the room, having disposed herself upon the yellow-striped settee.

At Nora's approach, Sir Frederick came toward her, his

hand outstretched. "My dear," he said, "it has been far too long since last we met."

"It has, indeed, sir."

He was a tall, almost gaunt gentleman with an aristocratic profile and thick, snow-white hair, and though his was still a formidable presence, there was now about him an aura of wounded strength. With her hand engulfed in both of his, Nora recalled that she had always admired the gentleman.

After welcoming Sir Frederick, Nora turned to his wife, who had risen to greet her nephew's widow. Lady Montgomery had always been shorter than Nora's own five feet four inches, but now she appeared even shorter, and so fragile that Nora hesitated to take her hand, afraid she might break the delicate bones.

As Nora had expected, the elderly couple still wore mourning for their grandson. Though the gentleman had seen fit to do no more than pin a black band around the sleeve of his dove-gray coat, the lady was dressed in unrelieved black from her tiny, booted feet to the small-crowned straw bonnet atop her head.

"I only just received your letter a half hour ago," Nora said, "for the post was taken to the manor house by mistake."

Offering no other excuse for having kept the older couple waiting, she let them decide what they would about Alicia's rudeness in not delivering the letter immediately. She did, however, apologize for her son's absence, explaining that Ceddy was being searched for.

"No doubt the boy is at play," Sir Frederick offered, a smile lurking in his alert brown eyes. "Who can blame him if he has no wish to be hauled home and scrubbed up just to make his bow to a set of relatives he cannot possibly recollect."

"Of course," his wife agreed. "At that age, our Alfred

was forever off on some lark or other, and no matter what the adventure, he always came home looking grubbier than a London street urchin.''

Because the recollection brought a smile to the lady's lips, Nora relaxed somewhat, heartened by the discovery that the Montgomerys found nothing shocking in a boy's disregard for cleanliness. "Please," she said, "will you not be seated?"

As soon as Nora disposed herself upon the small bench before the pianoforte, Sir Frederick took his place beside his wife on the settee, placing his hand over hers as if to lend her some of his strength. For several awkward seconds no one spoke. Because all three of them appeared to be on the alert, as if listening for an approaching footfall, Nora could only assume the older couple eagerly awaited their meeting with Ceddy—awaited it with an impatience that paralleled her own desire to keep the introduction from ever happening.

Unable to think what she should say to fill the uncomfortable void, she asked about the gentleman who was supposed to have accompanied them to Duddingham. "Your nephew, I believe you said in your letter. Was the gentleman unable to make the trip?"

Before replying to the question, Lady Montgomery exchanged looks with her husband. "No, no," she said, "Duncan came with us. He wanted to be at hand should we need any advice regarding the legalities of . . . of the adoption."

There! The word was out in the open, but if the previous silence had been difficult, the one that followed the utterance of that dreaded word was positively unnerving.

Into that intense quiet, Nora longed to scream her rejection of their proposal; to tell them in no uncertain terms that her son was not eligible for adoption, that she loved him too much to give him up. And yet, how could she deny Ceddy this opportunity? She had so little to offer him—nothing but her mother's heart—while his aunt and uncle could offer him wealth, an excellent education, and an undisputed place in the world.

Her lips trembled, and she had difficulty swallowing, for an obstruction had lodged in her throat threatening to choke her. "Sir Frederick," she said, "Lady Montgomery, I . . ." Tears spilled down her cheeks, and though Nora tried to brush them away with the back of her hand, they fell faster than she could banish them.

Sir Frederick moved to her side with a speed worthy of a much younger man. "My dear child," he said, offering her a snowy linen handkerchief, "forgive us. The subject was broached too precipitously. Time should have been allotted. Naturally, you will have questions. Possibly reservations. I—"

"No, sir," she replied, accepting the handkerchief and wiping her damp face. "I have no questions, and I fear that no amount of time would have sufficed to make this moment any easier." A quivery sigh caught in her throat. "Believe me, sir, I sincerely regret causing you further pain, you or Lady Montgomery, but it cannot be helped. Though I know it is not in my child's best interest to do so, I must keep him here with me. Therefore, I . . . I respectfully decline your offer to adopt Ceddy and make him your heir."

Chapter Three

Gemma could not, with any degree of civility, bid Mr. Duncan Jamison return to the cottage without her and Ceddy. Nor, she felt certain, would the disagreeable creature have done so even if she had been so bold as to ask. Therefore, they waited, neither speaking, while Ceddy tied his punt to the pier, then the threesome made their way back across the springy expanse of land, their ultimate destination the parlor where Nora and the Montgomerys waited.

As they circled around the stand of scrub, they all but bumped into Amos Littlejohn, who stood like a statue, waiting patiently. "I went to the windmill, like you said," Amos offered in lieu of a greeting. "Even though I knew Master Ceddy'd be at the river."

"And you were correct," Gemma replied. The servant would never know how much she wished that she had not gone to the river herself, especially when she recalled what she had done there—lifting her skirts and giving the detestable man beside her an uninterrupted view of her drawers.

The recollection brought a heated flush to her face, a flush she hoped no one would notice. "It appears I wasted both your time and mine, Amos. Next time, I will know better."

"Yes, miss," the orange-haired giant replied, stepping forward and doffing his cap to Gemma.

Obviously detecting the tension that existed between the young lady he had known all his life and the tall, slender stranger who stood beside her, Amos looked Duncan Jamison over from his curly-brimmed beaver to his elegant top boots, his manner not unlike that of a dog whose territory was in danger of invasion. Turning back to Gemma, he said, "You want I should draw the gentleman's cork, miss? Wouldn't be no trouble. No trouble at all."

At the suggestion, it was all Gemma could do to suppress the laugh that threatened to escape her throat, and when she snuck a look at the gentleman whose cork was in imminent danger, spying the surprised look upon his handsome face, she was obliged to press her fingernails into her palms to maintain a degree of composure. "Thank you, Amos, but I do not think there is a need for such drastic measures at this time. Mr. Jamison is some sort of cousin to Ceddy, and I am persuaded that Nora would consider it rude if you should do him an injury."

Amos gave the gentleman one last look, disappointment writ plainly upon his ruddy countenance. "Got to protect the ladies of the house," he said by way of explanation. "The mistress said that be part of my new job."

"And I see you take your job seriously," Mr. Jamison replied. To Gemma's surprise, he spoke quietly, calmly, his tone not in the least insulted. "Mrs. Westin is fortunate to have found such a conscientious protector. Well done. Amos, is it?"

When Amos smiled shyly at the compliment, then touched the bill of his cap respectfully, acknowledging the introduction, Gemma knew a desire to draw both their corks. Men! There was no understanding them. One minute they were ready to come to fisticuffs, and the next minute they acted as if nothing had happened.

Ceddy, too, was staring at the gentleman, all signs of his previous animosity gone. Now his eyes were wide with wonder. "Are we related, sir?"

"We are. But do not ask me the degree of our kinship, for I should need a genealogical chart to connect us accurately. However, I am pleased to number you among my relatives, and if you should like it once you come to know me a little, you may claim me as well." He extended his hand. "Duncan Jamison, at your service, Master Ceddy."

Ceddy shook the gentleman's hand with due gravity, but upon his young boy's face was every sign of dawning hero worship. "I knew I had a great-uncle, but I did not know I possessed any other male relatives. How do you do, Cousin Duncan?"

Gemma groaned inwardly. *Et tu, Brute?*

Deciding she would leave before she was obliged to witness further male camaraderie, Gemma strode purposefully toward the lane, where she noticed immediately that Sir Frederick's maroon-and-gold carriage was no longer in evidence. Concerned that something might have happened, and that Nora might have need of her, Gemma hurried toward the cottage, leaving the males to do what they would about Mr. Jamison's abandonment.

"Nora!" she called even before she entered the vestibule. "Where are you?"

"Here" came the reply.

Gemma followed the sound of her stepmother's voice and discovered her sitting at the top of the stairs. A lock of hair had worked its way from beneath the lace cap, and the lady held a gentleman's white handkerchief to her nose. Tears clung to her eyelashes.

A pain not unlike a sharp knife plunged itself into Gemma's heart, and with knees as wobbly as those of one who has actually sustained a knife wound, she climbed the stairs, stopping before Nora. "What happened?" she asked none too steadily. "Where are Sir Frederick and Lady Montgomery?"

Nora wiped away fresh tears. "I sent them away. I . . . I told them I could not let them adopt Ceddy."

The pain in Gemma's heart eased to a manageable throb. "Thank heaven."

She sat on the step beside Nora and took one of the lady's trembling hands, holding it between her own and offering what comfort she could, for Nora's tears still fell unchecked. "I am sorry you had such an unpleasant task, but it is behind you now, and we can resume our lives. Now we can forget this ever happened and go on just as before."

"Just as before?" Nora shook her head. "Surely you must see, my love, that we cannot continue as we were, for we still have not enough money to send Ceddy to school. Nor," she added, with a certain reticence, "have we sufficient funds to dress you as you deserve."

Gemma could only stare at this seeming non sequitur. "What foolishness is this? Am I not wearing a new dress at this very moment? And must I remind you that you refused to allow me to return the new bonnets I—"

"Frocks from a country dressmaker!" Nora interrupted. "You are Gemma Westin of Howarth Manor, and by right you ought to have already had your come-out, dressed in clothes befitting your station. You should be attending parties with other young people. At the very least, you should be going to the monthly assembly at the Blue Lion. Meeting young gentlemen."

"But I know all the gentlemen within a ten-mile radius, and I—"

"That is just it! There are no gentlemen of a suitable

age here in Duddingham. None save Mr. Newley, and though I should not say it, the curate is a rather dull fellow.''

"Very," Gemma agreed. "But what is this? Are you desirous of getting rid of me?''

Nora squeezed Gemma's hand in denial of the accusation. "You know better than that. I could not love you more if you were my own sister. I merely wish you to have the opportunity to form a suitable alliance. I would not have you spend your life never knowing the joys of true love, never experiencing the rewards of being a wife and mother.''

She resorted to the handkerchief once again, and this time sobs shook her body. "Oh, Gemma, forgive me, for I am the most selfish person in nature. I have just denied both you and Ceddy your one chance at a better life.''

When the three males reached the lane, and Duncan saw that the chaise and four were gone, he knew something untoward had occurred. His uncle Frederick was a man of punctilious manners, and he would not have abandoned his nephew for any but an important reason—a reason most likely involving Lady Montgomery's health and happiness.

Had the lad's mother come the ugly? Had she, indeed, asked for some exorbitant sum in return for her agreement to their plan?

"The coach be gone," Amos said, stating the obvious.

"Right you are. And now it would appear that I shall be obliged to find my own way to Howarth Manor, for I am to be the guest of Mr. and Mrs. Titus Westin.''

Duncan looked around him, searching for a stable, and though there was no such building in sight, he asked hopefully, "Is there a horse I might borrow?''

"Shank's mare," Amos replied affably. "That be the

only horse at the cottage. But there be cattle aplenty at the manor. You being a gentleman and all, do you but ask Mr. Titus Westin, he'll have one of the grooms saddle a horse for you."

Not wanting to argue the logic of saddling a horse once the destination was reached, Duncan thanked the giant and asked if he could direct him to the manor. "For if I must avail myself of Shank's mare, I should prefer to do so on the proper road."

"Sir," Ceddy said shyly, "I would be happy to show you the way."

"Good man!" he said. "Ought you to go inside to inform your mother of our destination, or may Amos perform that task for you?"

"I'll tell Mistress Westin," Amos agreed, then he touched his forelock and strode round the service tree, circling past the garden, his destination the rear of the cottage.

"Well, then, Ceddy," Duncan said, manfully refraining from taking so much as a glance at his once immaculate boots, their turned-over tops buff over black, "let us discover if my city legs can keep up with those of a lad reared in the country."

Had anyone bothered to ask, they would have discovered that Mr. Duncan Jamison was an avid participant in most of the sports enjoyed by the Corinthian set. As a result of his excellent physical condition, he covered the mile that separated Howard Cottage from the wrought-iron gates of the manor house without any apparent signs of discomfort, and only the most discerning observer would have noticed the subtlety with which the tall gentleman abbreviated his stride to accommodate that of the boy's much shorter legs.

As man and boy passed through the gates and strolled up the graveled carriageway that led to the stables, the gentleman remarked upon the beauty of the twelfth-century flint-and-mortar house. "But," he added, "though I knew the manor was Norman, I had no idea it was also moated. I believe such places are rare in this area."

"Yes, sir," Ceddy replied, a look of pride on his face for the place that had been his home for five years. "There is a moated castle about eight miles to the north of us, but it is nothing more than a ruin. Not a real home like the manor."

"You liked living here, did you?"

The boy nodded. "I do not remember ever living any-place else. Except for the cottage, of course," he added quickly, as if the oversight might be construed as disloyal.

"Of course."

"The manor was entailed," he offered in explanation, "so it went to Mr. Titus Westin. Papa Philip always said I was his son in every way that truly mattered, but the lawyers still gave the house to Titus and Alicia."

Duncan was interested to hear that bit of information regarding the relationship between Ceddy and Philip Westin, but he kept his thoughts on the subject to himself. Instead, he said, "An often unfortunate circumstance, entailment. However, since Jamison House, my father's estate, is entailed and will pass to me one day, I cannot totally dislike the practice."

The boy's brow was wrinkled in thought, as though he was considering the matter of entailment from a new perspective. "Do you live at Jamison House?"

"I grew up there, and I return to the estate for visits to my parents. For the most part, though, I reside in London, for my work is there."

"Have you a house in town?"

"No. I reside at the Albany, in a set left to me by my grandfather. The place is not particularly large, mind you, but it is conveniently located, and it suits the needs of a bachelor."

Ceddy pointed to a second-floor window in the far right corner of the house whose exterior was grayed with age. "That was my room," he said, a note of wistfulness in his voice. "It was not very big, either, but it had been Papa Philip's when he was a boy. When I came to live here, he gave the room to me."

They had reached the moat that surrounded the house, and when they stepped upon the thick iron bridge that was no longer drawn against enemy hordes but lay open at all times, they paused to look over the side. The moat had been drained and a portion of its depth and breadth filled in with tons of earth, and where once there had been water, now large, thick hawthorn bushes circled the house.

It being June, most of the pale pink blossoms were gone, with only one or two late bloomers in evidence, but if the hawthorn's gentle fragrance remained, it was overridden by the intoxicating aroma of roses. At the entrance to the house, massive rosebushes, the pure white of their flowers looking like newly fallen snow, climbed up and over the arched double doors.

While the hollow sounds of Duncan and Ceddy's footfalls still echoed beneath the iron bridge, the entrance doors to the manor house were thrown open and a very superior butler, his middle-aged face a study in displeasure, looked the two arrivals over from head to toe. Apparently, he did not like what he saw. Not that Duncan blamed him overmuch.

Duncan was not as neat as usual, having traversed the springy ground leading to the river, then adding to the dirt upon his boots by walking a mile in the dusty lane, but Ceddy was far from presentable. The boy's dark-blond hair was damp from the afternoon's activities and much in need of a good combing, and his shirt and nankeen breeches bore more than a hint of his enthusiasm for the river and the riverbanks.

The butler, not missing the least smudge or grain of dirt upon their persons, greeted them in a decidedly frosty manner. "Master Ceddy, what brings you here in such disarray? Is ought the matter?"

"Nothing is amiss, Ross. I have merely led my cousin, Mr. Jamison, to—"

"Mr. Jamison," the butler interrupted, unbending enough to incline his head in what passed for a bow. "Welcome, sir. Do come in, if you please."

After swinging the doors wide so that Duncan could enter the handsome vestibule with its black-and-white marble floor, the butler informed him that Mr. and Mrs. Westin were with Sir Frederick in the green drawing room, partaking of a light repast. "Though Lady Montgomery has chosen to have her tea in her bedchamber. I daresay the rigors of the journey were too much for her ladyship."

He took Duncan's hat and gloves, then asked if he might show him to the drawing room. "Master Ceddy," he added, "no doubt Cook will have something in the kitchen to tempt you before you return to the cottage. Providing, of course, you remove a layer of dirt before you sit down to table."

Having stiffened at the rebuff, Ceddy made Duncan a quick bow, then he turned and took a step toward the entrance.

"Do not go," Duncan said quietly, putting his hand on the boy's shoulder to stay his progress. "If you would not dislike it, I should like to take you up to meet your aunt Evelyn."

The butler cleared his throat meaningfully. "Your pardon, Mr. Jamison, but her ladyship—"

"I know, I know. The rigors of the journey. I shall inform her ladyship that you warned me. However, I believe the young man's presence might be just the tonic my aunt needs to lift her spirits."

"As you wish, sir."

Though his disapproval of such casual manners was evident in the slight lifting of his hawk's nose, the butler snapped his fingers to summon a footman who came at a run from someplace behind the grand staircase. "Wilson, show Mr. Jamison to her ladyship's suite."

"Yes, Mr. Ross. This way, sir."

The footman led them up the stairs, his manner as stiff as even the starched-up butler could have wished, but the instant they turned the corner to pass through to the east wing, he turned and winked at Ceddy. "You're a mite dirty there, Master Ceddy. Been catching trout, have you?"

When Ceddy smiled wide enough to show the gap in his teeth, Duncan gave the footman a nod of approval. "It is my suspicion," he informed the servant, "that the only thing Master Ceddy has caught today is 'what for' from the butler. The old stiff rump!"

After a startled moment, the footman so forgot himself as to laugh. "Coo ee. Isn't he just! A proper martinet is Mr. Ross, sir. It's not like the old days when Mr. Plimpton was butler here at the manor, and Mr. Philip Westin and the ladies were still in residence." After a sigh of resignation, he concluded his lament by saying, "No, sir, things ain't been the same since the ladies removed to the cottage."

Having arrived at the suite of rooms assigned to Lady Montgomery, the footman scratched politely at the door, then he stepped aside and allowed Duncan to announce himself.

"Aunt Evelyn?" Duncan said, spying the lady reclining on a daybed, a light robe across her lap and a large pillow to her back. "May we come in?"

"Duncan, my boy, please do. I should like to apologize for leaving you to find your own way, but after our interview, I was not feeling quite the thing, so your uncle . . ."

She stopped midsentence, for she had noticed that her nephew was not alone, and within moments, the look of polite interest upon her face gave way to an uncertain smile. "Duncan, is this . . . can this be Cedric?"

The lad made her a credible bow. "How do you do, Aunt?"

At the familial address, Lady Montgomery's smile grew, and she reached out a trembling hand to him, inviting him to come to her, not caring a fig that he was far too grubby to be in milady's chamber.

"Aunt Evelyn," Duncan said, remembering his manners a bit late, "allow me to present your great-nephew, who will have changed much since you saw him last."

She caught Ceddy's hand in hers, holding it fast, apparently unwilling to let it go. "He has, indeed, changed," she said, looking up at the healthy young boy who stood beside the daybed, "for he is no longer a babe. But I would have known him anywhere. He looks very like Charles when he was a lad."

"Did you know my father?"

Her ladyship nodded. "I knew him well. Charles was my sister's son, and I held him in great affection. And," she added, "I flatter myself that he was fond of me as well."

"He would have been hard to please had he not," Duncan replied.

"Was he tall?" Ceddy asked. "As tall as Cousin Duncan?"

The lady considered the question for a moment. "I cannot answer that accurately, for your father was six years older than Duncan, and the last time I saw them together, Duncan had not finished growing."

"I believe," Duncan said, "that I finally managed to exceed your father's height."

The boy tried manfully to hide his disappointment. "Oh," he said.

"But," Duncan continued quickly, "I was never able to

match his ability at games. A downy fellow was your father. It was he who taught me the proper use of the sword."

"My, yes," her ladyship added. "Charles was a born swordsman. And an excellent horseman as well."

"Was he?" Ceddy asked, his eyes bright with interest. "Please, ma'am, won't you tell me more?"

"I will, and gladly, my boy, but not just this moment. Before you arrived, I had just finished a cup of tea containing a soothing draught, and it is having its effect upon me, making me terribly sleepy. However, I shall see you tomorrow afternoon, for your mother has invited your uncle and me to call. We were hopeful of making your acquaintance at that time, but since that happy event has been accomplished today, you and I may meet tomorrow as old friends—the kind of friends who need not stand upon ceremony but may discuss anything they like with one another."

Duncan stepped forward and put his hand on Ceddy's shoulder, the pressure telling the lad to come away. "Tomorrow, then," he said, "at the cottage. Ceddy will see you there, Aunt Evelyn."

"Yes, ma'am," the boy replied, bowing politely, "I shall look forward to it. Until tomorrow, Aunt."

Gemma rose early the following day, her purpose to travel to Duddingham to speak with the attorney who handled her late father's estate. After lacing up her stoutest boots and fastening a serviceable dark-green spencer over an apple-green muslin dress, she tied the strings of her chip straw bonnet beneath her chin and set out to walk the three miles to the village.

The morning air was fresh and pleasantly warm upon her skin, and in the distance a meadow pipit encouraged her by its soft, musical song, but this was not a pleasure walk, so she was delighted when after little more than a mile, she was given a lift. The apothecary, Mr. Finn, an obliging old fellow whose antiquated dog cart and roan mare were often in evidence upon the lanes, had been called to the home of one of the Howarth Manor tenants and was now returning to his shop in the village.

"Jem Dobbs stepped into a badger hole," he said by way of greeting. "Been out to his place to set his leg."

"Poor man. I shall send Amos around this afternoon to see if Dobbs needs any wood or water brought in."

Mr. Finn tipped his hat. "Kind of you, Miss Westin. In the meantime, may I offer you a ride?"

"You certainly may, Mr. Finn, and I thank you."

Hoping this stroke of good fortune was an omen of things to come, Gemma lifted the hem of her skirt, gave the apothecary her hand, and let him assist her up onto the divided seat. With the roan mare trotting like a much younger animal, the remainder of the trip was accomplished in less than a quarter hour, so Gemma arrived at the lawyer's office only a few minutes after he had removed the "closed" sign from the door.

Mr. Eban Shaw rented an office on the floor above Madame Yvette's modiste shop, and as Gemma climbed the slender stairs just to the left of the colorfully decorated display window with its profusion of curled feathers and beads, she practiced the speech she had prepared the night before. It was imperative that she obtain a portion of her inheritance—at least enough to send Ceddy to school.

Unfortunately, though she presented her plan in a calm, logical manner, the lawyer's reaction soon convinced her that her earlier luck had deserted her.

"Out of the question!" Mr. Shaw declared in the unequivocal tones of one who handles the purse strings of a person he has known since her infancy. "Have you taken leave of your senses?"

The portly man pushed back his chair and stood, the exertion causing his pendulous jowls to reverberate like an aspic and his carefully combed hair to flop to the side of his head, revealing a large bald spot directly on top. Unaware of the tonsorial mishap, he rested his hands upon the ink-stained desk blotter and leaned forward. In this pose, he was practically looming over Gemma, who occupied the ladder-back chair on the other side of the desk.

"What woman's folly is this, madam? Have you not enough geegaws to suit you? Must you defy the wishes of the departed to satisfy your frivolous nature?"

"Sir!" Gemma said, rising as well, so that she was no longer in a position of subordination, "how dare you speak to me in this manner."

When the lawyer straightened, not a little taken aback by her unwillingness to be cowed, Gemma took a deep breath and let it out slowly, hoping the exercise might calm her anger. "I realize, Mr. Shaw, that you have been selected to execute my father's will, but that does not give you leave to malign me, or to belittle the seriousness of my request. If you have doubts as to my ability to handle such a sum, so be it. You need not hand the money over to me personally, merely—"

"On that, madam, we are of one mind, for I will not hand over so much as a shilling to you."

Ignoring his sarcasm, she continued. "You need only agree to pay the bills for my brother's school fees each term. Surely that is not too much to ask. It is, after all, my own money."

"Not," he countered, "unless the years have sped by faster than I have reckoned. You have not, I believe, reached your thirtieth birthday."

"Sir, you know I have not."

"Nor, I daresay, have you become betrothed or entered into the marriage state, in which instance I should be happy to turn the management of your funds over to your husband."

Gemma could feel the warmth in her cheeks. Because he had spoken thus, knowing it would embarrass her, she chose not to dignify the impertinent statement with a reply. Nonetheless, when a self-satisfied smile split his doughy face, Gemma knew a strong desire to reach across the desk and separate Mr. Eban Shaw from what remained of his pomaded hair.

"No husband, madam?" he asked. "No fiancé?"

"No."

"Then there is your answer. When you have reached the designated age, I shall hand over to you the three thousand pounds of your inheritance, plus interest earned. Until that day arrives, pray, do not waste my time again."

Chapter Four

Raging against men in general, and self-satisfied lawyers in particular, Gemma stomped down the narrow stairs leading from Eban Shaw's office, then flounced to the end of the high street. While she walked, she looked to neither right nor left, but headed directly for the old stone bridge that arched above the waters of the Nene.

Immersed in the depths of anger, she was in no mood to encounter anyone, especially not Mr. Duncan Jamison. "It wanted only this," she muttered when she recognized the gentleman who stood upon the bridge, gazing into the gently moving water as though it held the answer to some important question.

He leaned over the parapet, his elbows propped upon the centuries-old gray stone, and as a result of his stance, the blue coat and tan pantaloons of his riding attire strained against his surprisingly muscular physique. But it was not the barrister's muscles nor even his presence that caused the breath to catch in Gemma's throat, it was the handsome bay gelding that stood just this side of the bridge, his reins tied to the limb of a pear tree.

"Aries," she whispered.

It was her father's horse, and the unexpected sight of him standing there calmly munching grass brought back a flood of memories—memories that put all else from Gemma's mind.

Duncan felt rather than heard someone approach the bridge, and when he tore his attention from the river, he discovered the object of his troubled thoughts standing as if transfixed on the other side of the small bridge. "Good morning," he said politely. "You are abroad early, Miss Westin."

Apparently unaware that he had spoken, the young lady broke free of whatever had held her so still, then she covered the few yards that separated her from the handsome gelding the stable lad had saddled for Duncan earlier.

Taking hold of the animal's bridle, she blew softly into his nostrils. "Hello, Aries," she whispered. "How are you, old fellow?"

As if in answer, the horse pointed his ears forward and whickered, and while Duncan watched quietly, the lady buried her face in the animal's reddish-brown neck.

"I have missed you," she said. "Are they taking good care of you?"

"I can answer that one, ma'am."

She finally turned toward Duncan, and unlike their first meeting, this time there was no animosity in her eyes. Her look was unguarded, almost vulnerable, with traces of the affection she held for the horse still evident in those clear, sky-blue orbs, and for just a moment, Duncan wondered if it was possible to lose oneself in a woman's eyes.

"You can?"

"Can what?" he asked, still a bit dazed by what he had glimpsed in that unguarded moment.

"Aries," she said. "Are they taking good care of him?"

"Oh. Yes. Yes, of course," he replied, endeavoring to bring his attention back to the subject at hand. For some reason, his gaze had wandered to the lady's mouth. He had not noticed before what well-shaped lips she possessed; they were full and appeared quite soft, and he—"The, er, the stables are as clean and orderly as any horse, or horse owner, could wish for, and the groom who saddled the gelding did so in a manner that was both humane and capable."

Apparently satisfied with his answer, she asked nothing further, merely stroked Aries' forehead then stepped away, leaving the animal to his grazing.

"He was my father's mount," she said as she passed Duncan on the bridge.

For some reason he did not wish to ponder, Duncan did not want their meeting to end, so he hurried to the horse, untied the reins, and gave Aries a gentle tug, leading him until they caught up with the lady. "Are you bound for Howarth Cottage, Miss Westin?"

"I am, sir."

"May I accompany you? I am to meet my aunt and uncle there shortly."

"It is a public lane," she replied. "You may use it whenever you wish."

It was hardly a gracious invitation, but a barrister with political ambitions could not afford to be thin-skinned. Nor could a man who wished to gain control of this adoption situation. After getting to know young Ceddy a bit yesterday, and discovering the unquestionable devotion the lad felt for this woman he called his sister, Duncan had been obliged to rethink his initial impression of Miss Gemma Westin.

If it was at all likely that he had misinterpreted the comment he overheard yesterday, and the young lady had not actually bid the boy's mother seek ten thousand pounds in exchange for agreeing to the adoption, then it behooved Duncan to set the record straight, if only in his own mind. Should he find that she was the loving sister the boy thought her to be, then no harm done; however, if his first impression had been correct, and her only thought was for the money she might extort from the Montgomerys, then Duncan would know how to act.

He fell into step with her, the gelding on the lead, and only after they had crossed the bridge and covered at least a quarter mile at a quick, purposeful pace did it occur to him that she meant to walk the entire way. "How far is it to the cottage, ma'am?"

She did not look at him nor slow her step, but he thought he detected the tiniest twitch at the corner of her pretty mouth. "From here, sir, it is roughly three miles."

"How rough?"

When she was obliged to press her lips together to keep from laughing, he said, "With all this walking, I begin to suspect there is a conspiracy afoot, so to speak. A scheme aimed at testing my mettle as well as my boots."

She glanced at his highly polished Hessians, their silver tassels as yet unsullied. "A conspiracy, sir?"

"Yes, madam. If that is the case, I wish you would throw down the gauntlet in earnest, for if I am to be challenged, I should like the opportunity to purchase suitable footwear before the battle begins."

This time she forbore to look at him, and the amusement she could no longer contain found release in a quickly smothered chuckle.

"I heard that, madam."

Schooling her face to its previously sober demeanor, she said, "Heard what, sir?"

"That noise. It was either a chuckle or a gauntlet being dropped. Unfortunately, it did not last long enough for me to determine exactly which."

This time she laughed openly, and Duncan found the sound quite pleasing. As well, when she smiled, the motion caused that sprinkle of freckles across her nose and cheekbones to dance—a phenomenon that was not, he decided, an altogether unpleasant sight.

"Sir," she said a bit too airily to be trusted, "if you feel yourself unequal to the task of covering three miles of country lane, you may with a free conscience mount Aries and let the animal do all the work. Meanwhile, I, being made of sterner stuff, will continue this invigorating little ramble alone."

"Now that, madam, was a challenge if ever I heard one."

She chose to offer no comment, and as Duncan watched that smile appear a second time, he formed the opinion that freckles had definitely been given an unjust reputation. He was about to comment upon the subject when he heard the unmistakable pounding of hoofbeats behind them.

Turning to look over his shoulder, he saw a nondescript gray mare pulling a whiskey whose cane body had been all the crack twenty-five years ago when the gig was considered a sportsman's vehicle. Since that time, the equipage had fallen into the category of serviceable transportation, so it was not surprising that the young gentleman handling the ribbons wore the black hat and coat of a curate.

Miss Westin must have heard the approaching horse and gig, but she did not turn around. Instead, she kept her eyes forward, as though hoping the traveler would pass her by. Unfortunately, the curate did not take the hint; he hailed her loudly.

"Miss Westin. Yoo hoo, Miss Westin."

Duncan did not miss the muttered oath or the sigh

of resignation that escaped the lady, but he watched her summon a pleasant expression before she turned around. If he were to hazard a guess, he would have to say that Miss Gemma Westin was less than pleased to encounter the curate. But why? Did she have something to hide from the neighborhood spiritual leader?

"My dear Miss Westin," the man began even before the mare came to a complete stop. "What a pleasure to see you on this sunny morning."

"Mr. Newley," she said, curtsying.

Sweeping off his hat, he sketched her a bow, then he raised his voice much like an actor on a stage. "Dear lady, if I may borrow from the Psalmist, chapter fifty, verse 2, you are 'the perfection of beauty.' I actually pity the sunshine, for its rays pale when compared to your bright smile. Likewise, the blue of the sky fades when compared to your eyes, and the blush of the rose wanes when near your cheek."

After being obliged to endure that overblown speech, the lady's cheeks most definitely outblushed the rose, but apparently the parson did not notice her discomfort. "You will be wondering, my dear Miss Westin, why I am on the road at such an early hour. 'Twas the work of providence, for I chanced to see you on the stairs outside Mr. Eban Shaw's place of business, and I said to myself, 'Bascombe Newley, if Miss Westin has been visiting her father's lawyer, depend upon it, the matter will be of some importance.'

"Then," he continued, "when I saw you walk away from the village in such haste, I decided that it behooved me to follow you, in the event you should be in need of a wiser head to help you sort out any business that might have been beyond your understanding."

The lady stiffened, and while Duncan pondered the nature of the business that had taken her out so early in the day to consult with her attorney, the curate waited as if expecting confirmation of Miss Westin's need for a wiser head. Though no such substantiation was forthcoming, the parson persevered.

"Since it was my intention to visit Jem Dobbs later in the day—Jem stepped in a badger hole, don't you know—I sent my man to the smithy's at a run to fetch my gig, which is why you see me before you in such good time. I am at your service, my dear madam."

"Mr. Newley," Miss Westin said, pointedly not thanking the fellow for his offer, "pray allow me to introduce Mr. Duncan Jamison of London."

As if only just noticing that the lady was not alone, the curate gave Duncan his full attention, blinking his eyelids in a manner that put the London gentleman in mind of a barn owl, so much so that he would not have been surprised by a whoo whoo?

The parson was a smallish man, not much taller than Miss Westin, and so thin the term spindle shanks might have been coined for the purpose of describing him. Though he was young, no more than twenty-seven years old, his expression was pedantic enough to serve for a man twice his age.

"Mr. Newley," Duncan said, bowing politely.

"Sir," the curate said, inclining his head. "London, eh?" Without waiting for a reply, he lifted his voice again. " 'I am a stranger with thee, and a sojourner.' *Psalms,* chapter thirty-nine, verse twelve."

Duncan could not have been more surprised if the fellow had struck him, and the fact that he was unaccustomed to having Scripture quoted at him must have shown on his face, for Miss Westin was having difficulty preserving her countenance.

The recitation obviously at an end, the curate reached his hand down to the lady. "Come, my dear Miss Westin, allow me to take you up, for I am persuaded you cannot wish to walk all the way to Howarth Cottage.''

She did not take the proffered hand. "Thank you, Mr. Newley, but I could not be so rude as to abandon Mr. Jamison. He is . . ." She paused, as if searching her mind for a plausible excuse to avoid Young Spindle Shank's escort, and Duncan surprised himself by supplying her need.

"I am new to the area," he said, "and am hopelessly lost. Miss Westin was so good as to volunteer to guide me back to Howarth Manor, where I am staying for a few days."

The curate's expression went from owlish to mulish. "The solution to both dilemmas is quite clear, sir. Miss Westin may ride with me in the gig, while you follow us on horseback."

The man did not add, "Breathing my dust," but the glint in his eyes spoke for itself. He obviously considered Miss Westin to be private preserves, and he wanted no poaching.

"Miss Westin," he repeated, his tone insistent.

Accepting the inevitable with as much grace as possible, the lady lifted the hem of her skirt in preparation to climb aboard the gig. Before she could take the curate's out-stretched hand, however, Duncan stepped beside her, put his hand beneath her elbow, and assisted her into the vehicle.

As he suspected, the whiskey had been built to accommo-date only one person, and even though Newley was bony, the lady was obliged to wedge herself into a space barely large enough for a small child. Since her distaste for the forced intimacy was writ plainly upon her face, Duncan gave up wondering why she had hoped the curate would drive on by without stopping. Obviously, the parson wished for some private time in which to fix his interest with her, and just as obviously, she hoped to depress his enthusiasm before it came to an open declaration of his intention.

Why, Duncan wondered, did she not give the fellow the set down he deserved and be done with it? After all, a young lady as pretty as Miss Westin must have more prospects than Young Spindle Shanks. Even if she did not, surely there was no pressure being placed upon her to accept such a jackanapes. Or was there?

The curate lifted the reins, and after casting Duncan a smug look unbefitting a man of the cloth, he gave the mare the office to proceed. Within seconds he had whipped the animal into a gallop, and soon the gig was traveling at breakneck speed down the lane. Duncan was left to mount the gelding and follow the vehicle, inhaling the parson's dust all the way to the cottage.

Once the distance was covered, however, Duncan wiped the smug look from Newley's face by dismounting, tossing Aries' reins over a limb of the service tree, and going immediately to assist Miss Westin to alight. Without asking, or receiving permission, he caught the young lady round her slim waist and lifted her down, taking his own sweet time before setting her on her feet. Moments later, after he had tucked her arm in his, he nodded dismissal to the curate.

"No need to get down, Newley. I will see Miss Westin safely inside."

Safely inside? Gemma doubted she would ever feel safe again. For those few minutes when the whiskey had careened over the rough lane, and she had clung with both hands to the fragile cane seat, she had feared she might be thrown to her death. She had been convinced that nothing could steal her breath away as that wild ride had done, but she was obliged to revise her opinion when Mr. Duncan Jamison put his strong hands around her waist and swung her free of the gig.

She had expected him to take her arm as he had done before and steady her while she jumped down, but he ignored her outstretched hand. To her surprise, he caught her firmly by the waist, causing every last ounce of breath to forsake her lungs, and while his eyes held hers, he slowly lifted her to the ground, delaying the action longer than was necessary, prolonging it until she thought she might faint from lack of air.

He bore her weight as though it were negligible, and when he finally allowed her feet to touch the ground, she stood there for what seemed an eternity, too bemused to recall the necessary procedure for replenishing her lungs. It was fortunate for the continued health of that vital organ that Gemma chanced to see something pass between the two men—something that snapped her out of her bemusement and prompted her to draw in a big gulp of air.

Upon Mr. Newley's face was an expression of resentment at having been bested, while the smile on Mr. Jamison's lips was one of triumph. The entire incident—the mad gallop, as well as the slow, highly improper lifting down from the gig—had been nothing more than a contest between males, and *she* merely the object over which they fought. Calling herself a fool for having reacted like the veryest ninnyhammer over the feel of a man's hands upon her person, she yanked her arm free of Mr. Jamison's and hurried up the flagstone path. She neither knew nor cared when Mr. Newley took himself off.

"Miss Westin," Mr. Jamison called after her. "Please wait."

She did not wait, but continued up the path, and when he caught up with her beside the rose arbor, he stepped in front of her to block her way. "Did I do something to offend you?" he asked. "If so, please allow me to apologize, for I had no wish to—"

"Save your apologies, Mr. Jamison. I assure you I want no part of them. Considering our conversation by the bridge, I should not have been surprised when you accepted a challenge, no matter how foolish. In the future, however, if you must involve yourself in dangerous contests, I pray you will do so at a time when I am not caught in the middle."

"You are right, of course, ma'am, and I do most humbly beg your—"

"I told you," she said, her voice icy, "that I wanted no part of your apologies. Now step aside, sir, and let me pass."

At first she thought he meant to insist she hear him out, but he must have thought better of it. "As you wish," he said, his voice every bit as cool as hers. After making her an exaggerated bow, he moved aside to give her ample room to pass, and in doing so, his knee hit against the wrought-iron bench beneath the rose arbor, a circumstance that obliged Gemma to turn her back to him to hide her smile.

Expecting to hear him retrace his steps to the lane and mount the gelding he had left tied to a limb of the tree, she was surprised to be privy to a muttered oath, one no gentleman had ever before voiced in her presence. The word so startled her that she turned to stare at him, and what she saw put all else from her mind. Mr. Jamison was down on one knee, bending over something hidden from her sight by the thickness of the climbing roses.

"Miss Westin," he said, his voice brooking no argument, "your servant, Amos, find him immediately and send him to the village to fetch the doctor."

"Duddingham has no doctor, sir, only Mr. Finn, the apothecary. But what is the matter? Have you injured yourself?"

"It is not I," he said.

"If not you, sir, then who?"

When he did not answer, she said, "If it is your purpose to frighten me, Mr. Jamison, allow me to inform you that you are succeeding. And I do not like it."

He gave little evidence of having heard her comment, for while she had been busy giving him a piece of her mind, he had been occupied in scooping something up into his arms. Moments later, when he straightened and turned toward her, Gemma's knees threatened to give way beneath her, for the something he carried was Ceddy.

The boy neither moved nor made a sound. His eyelids were closed, his usually animated face was deathly pale, and his head fell back limply against Mr. Jamison's arm. Most frightening of all, though, were the moist, dark-red stains that seemed to cover the entire front of the lad's shirt.

"Do not just stand there!" Mr. Jamison ordered. "Do as I told you, for we need the apothecary. Young Ceddy has been shot."

Chapter Five

"Amos!" Gemma shouted the instant she reached the vestibule. "Amos! Come quickly. I have need of you."

"Gemma, my love," Nora called from the top of the stairs, "what is amiss? Are you all . . ."

The question died upon her lips when she spied Mr. Jamison in the doorway, her injured son in his arms. For no more than the space of a moment she swayed as though she might faint, but instead of succumbing to the fear that gripped her, she caught hold of the banister to steady herself. "Ceddy," she said, the word half sob. "Is he—"

"The boy is unconscious, ma'am, but it appears he has lost a great deal of blood. More than that, I cannot say."

"Of course you cannot," Nora said, visibly pulling herself together by sheer force of will. "If you please, sir, bring my son up to his room. He will be more comfortable on his own bed."

While the gentleman took the stairs two at a time, Amos Littlejohn came from the kitchen, followed closely by both the cook and the maid of all work. At the sight of the injured boy, the cook gasped and blessed herself, and the maid pulled her apron up over her face and began to weep. Only Amos remained quiet.

"Hush," Gemma ordered the maid. "This is no time for hysterics. If you cannot keep your wits about you, go back to the kitchen, for I must speak with Amos, and he must be able to hear me."

Amos stepped forward, and though his face was almost as white as Ceddy's, he appeared calm. "What you want I should do, Miss Gemma?"

"Go for Mr. Finn," she told him. "I saw him this morning, and at that time his destination was the village. Should you not find him in his shop, ask if anyone knows where he may be found. If no one knows his whereabouts, try at Jem Dobbs's cottage, for he was at Jem's earlier."

"Not to worry, miss. I'll find Mr. Finn. I'll not return until I do."

He took off at a run and was halfway to the lane before Gemma stopped him. "Amos! Wait." She pointed to Aries, who stood patiently beside the service tree. "Take the horse. It will be quicker."

Amos looked from her to the gelding, then back again. "But Aries b'aint ours no more, miss. He belongs to Mr. Titus Westin, and the new mistress be powerful angry if she know I took to riding their cattle. Likely she'd have me up on charges."

"Take the horse," Gemma repeated. "If charges are brought against anyone, it will be Mr. Titus Westin, for I have no doubt this day's work can be laid directly at his door. Titus is the only person allowed to hunt on the estate, and we all know what an atrocious shot he is."

Amos touched his finger to his forelock, then he untied the gelding's reins, sprung into the saddle, and galloped off toward the village. The dust of the lane was still swirling about, churned up by Aries' hooves, when Gemma turned to look in the direction of the manor house.

Not bothering to lower her voice, she said, "I warn you, Titus Westin, if that boy dies, I will see you pay dearly."

As ill luck would have it, her vow did not go unheard, for Duncan stood at the open window looking down upon the garden and her. He had moved to the side of the bedchamber to be out of the way, yet close at hand if he should be needed, and the lady's words had traveled upward with surprising clarity.

After he had carried Ceddy upstairs, Duncan had waited only until the mother pulled back the counterpane before he laid the lad gently upon the bed. Since Mrs. Nora Westin had not seen fit to give way to a bout of hysterics, Duncan did as she bid him and moved aside so she could tend to the boy's needs.

From a chamber he supposed must be her own, she had fetched a woven work basket containing scissors, rolls of bandage, and some ointments, and though her hands shook, her fingers moved with competence as she cut away the bloody shirt from the boy's still unmoving body. It was while she pressed a thick pad of bandage against what appeared to be a bullet hole in the lad's shoulder that Duncan turned to look out into the lane where he heard voices raised.

He watched Amos mount the gelding and gallop toward the village, then he heard Miss Westin vow to make Titus Westin pay should anything happen to Ceddy.

Pay in what way? With his life? His freedom? His money?

Twenty-four hours ago, Duncan would have had little doubt which would be the forfeit. Money. Now, of course, he was less certain. He had had an opportunity for a closer look at both the women involved in Ceddy Creighton's life, and unless he was mistaken in his reading of their characters, Nora Westin and Miss Gemma Westin loved the boy.

The boy's mother had refused to allow the Montgomerys to adopt Ceddy, giving as her reason her unwillingness to have him taken from the estate. "I must keep him here with me," she had said.

Because Mrs. Westin had been crying, Sir Frederick had not asked her why she did not wish the lad removed from the place, but it had been his intention to seek the answer when they met today. With Ceddy lying wounded—who knew how seriously?—Duncan doubted the answer would be forthcoming this day.

"Mr. Jamison," Nora Westin said, bringing his attention back to her, "will you be so kind as to fetch Sir Frederick and Lady Montgomery? If . . . if anything should . . ." She was obliged to take a deep breath before she continued. "What I mean to say is, they should have the choice of being here if they wish. Ceddy is their great-nephew, and it is only right that they be here."

"I will fetch them, ma'am. Just as soon as the apothecary arrives."

"Mother?"

At the sound of the weak voice, Nora turned quickly to look at her son, and Duncan crossed the room in three long strides. The boy's face had regained a bit of its color, and his eyes were open. His mother made a gulping sound, as though swallowing a sob. "Ceddy," she whispered.

"How do you feel, lad?" Duncan asked.

The boy blinked, then, as if regaining all his senses, he cried out, "Ouch! Mother, you are hurting me. Must you press so hard?"

Nora Westin uttered a sound that was part laughter and part tears, then she relaxed her pressure, lifting the bandage to see if the bleeding had stopped. "I am sorry," she said, sounding every inch the mother, "but you are still bleeding just a little, and I must do what is needed."

"Ceddy," Duncan said, "if you feel up to it, can you tell us who shot you?"

"I do not know, Cousin. I never saw anyone."

"No one at all?"

"No, sir."

"Where were you?"

"Across the lane, on the far side of that stand of scrub. Mother had told me not to get dirty, for my aunt and uncle were to come for tea, so I knew better than to go to the river."

He looked rather sheepishly at his mother. "Yesterday I found a bird's nest out in the open, with two hatchlings inside. Greenfinches, I believe they were, and the chicks were chirping like anything for their mother."

When no one seemed angry with him, nor bid him speak no more, the lad continued. "I had no idea where the nest had come from, but I knew if it remained unprotected, some animal would come along and think he had found breakfast. Not sure what I should do, I took the nest and wedged it securely in the branches of one of the scrubs. I went this morning to see if the mother bird had found them."

"And had she?" Duncan asked.

"I had not yet reached the nest when I heard the gunfire. An instant later I felt an unbelievable burning in my right shoulder, and when I saw the blood begin to soak my shirt, I knew I had better get home as fast as possible."

He looked from his mother to Duncan. "I do not remember much after that. Did I make it all the way to the cottage?"

"You made it as far as the rose arbor, my boy. That is where I found you. You had lost consciousness, so I carried you up here to your chamber."

"Thank you, sir. Lucky for me you were nearby, for I doubt my mother or Gemma could have carried me up the stairs."

"Think nothing of it, Ceddy, I—"

He got no further, for the boy's mother had begun to tremble all over, and if Duncan had not caught her, she would have fallen to the floor. He laid her across the foot of her son's bed, then he went to the window and called down to Miss Westin, who was pacing up and down the flagstone path, as if willing the apothecary to appear.

"Ma'am. Mrs. Westin has need of you."

She looked up at him, the tearstains on her cheeks evident even at a distance. "Ceddy? Is he . . ."

"The boy is fine. He is conscious and the bleeding has been stanched. But now that he has come around, it is his mother who has fainted."

"An odd occurrence, this shooting," Mr. Titus Westin said, sitting on the edge of one of the brocade chairs that gave the green withdrawing room its name. "Very odd indeed."

Their host looked most uncomfortable, but his discomfort had nothing to do with the day's events. It was obvious to both the other gentleman in the room that he dared not sit back, for his white marcella waistcoat was already straining across his sizable paunch, and it looked as though the least added pressure might well send the large gold buttons flying across the room.

"Unfortunate, too, of course," Titus continued, "but odd all the same, for we have had very little trouble with poachers on the estate. I spoke to my gamekeeper, and the fellow promises to be more vigilant in the future. A good thing the boy was not seriously injured."

When their host signaled the butler, who stood unobtrusively on the far side of the drawing room, to bring the sherry decanter and refill his glass, Sir Frederick leaned over to say a private word to his nephew. "If you ask me, Duncan, this entire episode has a rummish smell to it."

"Quite rummish, sir."

"After you left the cottage, did you find an opportunity to go by the scene of the shooting?"

"I did."

"What did you discover?"

Before he answered the question, Duncan glanced at their host to assure himself that the man's attention was still fixed upon the replenishing of his wineglass. "Using the drops of blood on the ground as my guide, it was easy to determine just where the boy was standing when he was shot."

"Was he hidden from view, at least enough so that any movement might prompt a poacher to mistake him for game?"

Duncan shook his head. "The lad was in plain sight. There was no way he could have been mistaken for anything but what he is, a medium-sized boy. Poacher or hunter, whoever pulled the trigger was either in his cups or blind."

"Or out for mischief."

The two men exchanged troubled glances. "As you say, Uncle."

They were obliged to delay further discussion of the subject, for at that moment the door to the drawing room was opened by a footman, and Lady Montgomery entered, followed by their hostess, Mrs. Alicia Westin. As usual, Lady Montgomery wore black, but their hostess had chosen for the occasion a dress of ruby-red satin—a dress whose style and low neckline were more suitable to the ballroom than to an evening at home with only one's husband and three guests in attendance.

Alicia, as she had begged them to call her, was a beautiful woman with alabaster skin and pouting lips, and though she was about the same age as the previous lady of the manor, she possessed neither Mrs. Nora Westin's charm nor her style. Aside from the provocative red dress that revealed a startling amount of her voluptuous figure, she had chosen to arrange her dusky curls in a profusion of ringlets and fastened a diamond necklace around her creamy throat.

"Mr. Jamison," she drawled, lowering her dark lashes, then raising them slowly, in a way that left Duncan in no doubt of her desire to become better acquainted with him, "I bid you good evening. And Sir Frederick. I hope I see you well, sir." To her husband, who was still struggling to stand at the ladies' entrance, she vouchsafed not a word.

Since both the ladies refused the offer of sherry, Titus gave his arm to Lady Montgomery and led the party across the vestibule and into the dining room, where the mahogany table was set with enough silver and crystal to impress a duke. The guests had only just taken their places, with Sir Frederick to the hostess's right and Duncan to her left, when the footman scratched at the door. After whispering something in the butler's ear, the servant placed a visiting card in the chased silver salver at the end of the buffet, then he stepped back to await further orders.

Availing himself of the small tray, the pompous butler walked to the foot of the table and bowed to Alicia. "Madam, a gentleman sends his compliments to you and asks if he might be allowed to pay his respects to Sir Frederick and Lady Montgomery."

"What nonsense is this?" Titus said from the far end of the long table. "No gentleman would have the effrontery to call at this hour, not even in the country. What the devil does this fellow mean by presenting himself at my door just as we are sitting down to our mutton?"

Alicia cast an icy look at her husband, then she smiled sweetly at the silver-haired gentleman to her right. "I am persuaded, Sir Frederick, that you will know best if this gentleman should be granted his wish to speak with you."

"May I see the card?"

The butler walked around to present the salver to Sir Frederick, who read the name printed upon the paste-board square. "Well," he said, looking across the table at his nephew, "this is a surprise indeed. It seems your cousin Nevil is here."

"La, sir," Alicia said, tapping her fan playfully against the sleeve of Mr. Nevil Montgomery's well-cut plum-colored coat, "I believe you are making sport of me."

"Never," said the gentleman, a practiced smile upon his handsome face.

"But the very idea of Prinny falling to his knees before Lady Bessborough and declaring his undying love, why, 'pon my soul, 'tis too droll by half."

"But nonetheless true, Mrs. Wes—"

"Please," she said, "call me Alicia."

The lady and gentleman were taking a turn around the drawing room while the other members of the party played a hand of loo, and since no one seemed to be interested in their conversation, Nevil lowered his voice to a whisper. "Alicia," he drawled. "A beautiful name for a beautiful lady. Were I a poet, I should set it to verse."

"But I vow, sir, it rhymes with nothing."

"I beg to differ, fair madam. The difficulty lies only in the fact that you cannot see yourself as a man would see you, see you and be inspired by your beauty. *Alicia's eyes . . . delicious sighs.* The possibilities are endless."

Once again, the lady tapped him with her fan, and though she bid him behave himself, the smile upon her usually pouty lips gave the lie to the command. "The story," she said. "Tell me what happened between Prinny and his latest flirt."

"Nothing much, actually. Rumor has it that Lady Bessborough finally convinced the prince that they could never be more than friends, and they parted on the best of terms. Of course, the final and most thought-provoking part of this entire fiasco has all of London placing wagers. Just how, everyone wishes to know, did her ladyship manage to get her elephantine swain up off his knees?"

The lady and gentleman laughed aloud, apparently deriving much pleasure from the story and from one another's company. It was not to be wondered at, of course, for Mr. Nevil Montgomery was adept at these little flirtations; they kept him a favorite among the less formal hostesses in town. With none of his barrister cousin's connections, and nothing near Mr. Jamison's wealth, Nevil depended upon his extraordinary good looks and practiced charm to keep him in country house invitations the year round—invitations that helped him stretch his meager income.

"Speaking of rumors," he said, as they continued their stroll, "the word at the Blue Lion, where I am put up for the next day or so, awaiting the arrival of my friends, is that my cousin, Mr. Duncan Jamison, figures as something of a hero. I heard that he saved a young boy from the brink of death this very day. Is that true? Was the lad's injury serious?"

"Pshaw," Alicia replied, ennui creeping into her voice. "The boy has an injured shoulder, nothing more, and other than being obliged to keep his arm in a sling for a few days, he came to no harm."

"What good fortune, to be sure. How came the youngster to be hurt? Does anyone know?"

"All I know, sir, is that I am heartily sick of the entire subject."

Nevil caught her fingers and lifted them to his lips in apology. "Boredom," he said, "is the one unforgivable sin, and I should hate it to get back to the friends who are to meet me here later in the week that I had a beautiful and most desirable woman all to myself and could find no subject that pleased her. Perhaps," he continued, his voice soft and caressing, "if I am ever this way again, I might think of more *on dits* to amuse you."

Finding this conversation more to her liking, Alicia was struck with a happy thought. "Sir, pray allow me to send a servant to the village for your things. If you must cool your heels until your friends arrive to take you on to their hunting box, why not spend that time here at Howarth Manor, where you are among family."

"And new friends," he added, lifting her fingers for another kiss. "Quite charming new friends."

The next two days were as inclement as the previous week had been sunny. The skies seemed to have opened up for good, dumping hours of unceasing rain upon the countryside, thereby turning the roads to quagmires and making them all but unusable. If there was a good side to this deluge, it was that the rain enabled the ladies of Howarth Cottage to keep Master Ceddy within doors where he could do no harm to his healing shoulder. Unfortunately, there was also a bad side, dealing with the lad's growing boredom.

Of course, Gemma was heartily sick of the weather herself. For as long as she could remember, being restricted to the house had given her a restless feeling, but she soon discovered that being confined to an area no larger than the cottage was doubly difficult to endure.

"Will this rain never stop," she said, tossing aside the book of poetry whose page had not been turned for the last hour. "I believe I shall go mad if I am obliged to spend another day indoors."

"Not you, too," Nora said, laying her embroidery upon the worktable. "First Ceddy, now you. I see how it is. If I am to have any peace around the place, I shall be obliged to tie the two of you back to back, like a brace of partridge, and wrap kerchiefs around your mouths."

"Mother!" exclaimed her son from the well-worn rose-colored settee upon which he rested, "you would not."

"She *could* not," Gemma said.

Rising quickly from her chair, Gemma struck a pose, placing her hands upon her hips and spreading her feet wide apart much as she had seen villains do on the stage. Trying for a deep voice, she said, "Fear not, young sir, for the wench cannot subdue me. I am both taller and stronger than she, and if there is to be any mayhem committed this day, *I* shall be the perpetrator and yonder wench shall be the perpetratee."

The boy giggled. "What say you to that, Mother?"

"I say, 'Ha!'"

Nora rose and took a similar stance, her hands upon her hips. "I am a woman grown, and no slip of a girl can make a perpetratee of me. Not while I have my wits about me. With my keen senses, I shall surely outsmart the braggart."

"You would do better," Ceddy suggested, "if you had a sword. Then you could run her through."

"My thoughts exactly," Nora declared. "What think you, Ceddy, do you suppose you could help me make such a weapon?"

"If he cannot do so, ma'am," said a genuinely deep voice, "I beg you will accept my services."

"Cousin!" Ceddy shouted.

Gemma wheeled around and came face-to-face with Mr. Duncan Jamison, who stood in the arched doorway, dressed in an old rubberized coat and hat that looked very like the ones her father used to wear. Mortified to have been caught playing the fool, she said, "Sir, this is a surprise."

"But a most welcome one," Nora added, going to him, her hands outstretched as if to an old friend. "I am delighted to see you, sir, for now that I have had a few days to calm my overwrought senses, I wish to tell you just how much in your debt we all are."

Mr. Jamison took Nora's hands in his, but he refused to accept her words of gratitude. "I assure you, ma'am, you owe me nothing. I only hope you will forgive me for intruding upon your fun. I knocked at the front door, but the rain is making such a racket, it must have covered the sound."

"You could never intrude, sir. Please, come join us." When he hesitated, she said, "Or perhaps we might all go into the drawing room. I fear this little parlor is rather shabby for receiving guests."

The gentleman looked about him at the cozy room with its worn upholstery and the array of books and puzzles stacked about on the floor. "This room perfectly suits my tastes, Mrs. Westin, and if you will allow it, I will join you here once I have rid myself of this sodden coat and hat. And," he added with a grin, "should you not forbid such familiarity, I believe it would be prudent of me to remove my boots. I walked from the manor, and I am all over mud."

Happy to be quit of the scene of her embarrassment, Gemma hurried to the kitchen to bid Amos come take their caller's things.

"Nuncheon be almost ready, Miss Gemma," Cook informed her. "Shall I have Daisy set a place for the gentleman?"

Good manners, plus a pretty good notion of what Nora

would reply to that question, obliged Gemma to answer in the affirmative. "And if we have anything in the house suitable for a gentleman to drink, you might serve that as well."

"We've naught but ale, miss, and a few bottles of my own brambleberry wine."

Since Gemma could well imagine what a gentleman accustomed to dining at the most exclusive tables in London, and partaking of the finest burgundy, madeira, and claret, would say if served homemade wine, she chose the ale.

Unable to think of a valid reason to linger in the kitchen, Gemma returned to the little sitting room, where she found Mr. Jamison, *sans* boots, lounging comfortably beside Ceddy on the settee. When he would have stood at her entrance, she bid him remain seated.

"Look, Gemma," Ceddy said, "Cousin Duncan brought me a telescope."

"Actually, my boy, I am but the messenger. It was your uncle who brought the instrument to Suffolk. I believe it belonged to his grandson some years ago."

Mr. Jamison took the brass-trimmed glass and extended it to its full length, then he quit the settee and walked over to the open window. After putting the viewing end of the instrument to his eye, he made a few minor turning adjustments to a center section of the glass, then he called Ceddy over and handed him the telescope. "Take a look at the service tree, near its base. I believe you will be able to see the red head of a cardinal beetle."

Ceddy did as he was bid, then, with his right eye squeezed shut and his mouth agape, he exclaimed, "By Jupiter! I see the beetle, Cousin. It is just as clear. So clear I almost believe myself standing close enough to lift the insect right off the tree."

"What a splendid gift," Nora said, "and one made even

more welcome by its delivery at such an opportune time. For I must tell you, Mr. Jamison, that my son has read every book and worked every last picture puzzle in the house, and now he finds himself with nothing left to do."

The gentleman turned away from the window. "Sir Frederick suspected as much. He would have brought the telescope to the boy himself had the rain not made travel almost impossible for one of his age."

Recalling his manners, Ceddy said, "Thank you for coming in such bad weather, Cousin."

"Not at all, my boy. Your uncle thought you might be growing bored with your forced inactivity, so he asked me to deliver the telescope to you with his compliments."

"It was very good of Sir Frederick," Nora said. "And most intuitive, for boredom seems to be the word of the day here at Howarth Cottage. It is like a disease, and I fear we are all infected by it."

Some imp inside Gemma prompted her to say, "I hope, Mr. Jamison, that you may not catch the disease from us."

To her surprise, the gentleman laughed. "Are you quite certain, Miss Westin, that you do not hope I *may* catch it?"

Not waiting for her answer, he said to Ceddy, "I believe Miss Westin just issued a challenge, my boy. One no sportsman could, in good conscience, refuse."

"Challenge?" Gemma said. "I did no such—"

"Ergo, Ceddy, it is my suggestion that we form teams, the men against the ladies. We shall play such games as are appropriate to both the sexes and ascertain who can best withstand this virulent outbreak of boredom."

His teammate agreed with enthusiasm. "Excellent, sir! Men against the ladies. A capital idea, is it not, Gemma?"

The best Gemma could do by way of an answer was a halfhearted smile. She was torn. On the one hand, she wanted to thank Duncan Jamison for raising Ceddy's spirits, and on the other hand, she desired to give the man a proper set down for bringing up the subject of challenges. She had not forgotten that crazy ride in Mr. Newley's gig, nor had she forgotten the way she reacted when Mr. Jamison lifted her down from the whiskey, his strong hands about her waist. That particular memory had robbed her of sleep the past two nights, and now it sent the warmth of embarrassment stealing up to her cheeks.

"But what shall we play, Cousin? I . . . I do not know any grown-up games."

"There are no grown-up games, my boy. Only grown-up people who play children's games. Now, what have you in the house? I will play anything but loo." He lifted his hand as if to stop the lad from suggesting the game. "Do not, I beg of you, ask me to sit through another hand of loo."

Nora laughed. "Is that how the occupants of the manor have been keeping themselves entertained?"

Mr. Jamison gave her a look that spoke volumes. "I would hardly call it entertainment, ma'am. More like penance. Especially if one is obliged to partner Mr. Titus Westin."

Encouraged by a chuckle from Nora, he continued. "I should not like to speak ill of one who is a close connection of yours, ma'am, but—"

"Regretfully," Gemma said, "*I* am the only person in the room who must admit to being related to Titus, and I give you leave to speak as ill of him as you wish."

"Never tell us," Nora interrupted, concern upon her face, "that Titus plays deep."

"No, ma'am, we played for mere chicken stakes."

"I collect," Gemma said, "that Mr. Jamison is hesitant to state the obvious, that Titus has no head for the game."

"No head for it? Madam, the man plays so badly he should not even be allowed to own a deck of cards."

Nora and Gemma both laughed. "As bad as that?" Nora asked.

"Worse, ma'am. He could never, and I do mean never, remember which suit was trump. And you will find this difficult to believe, but twice he used Pam to take a trick when he held suitable cards of that trump in his hand."

While Nora tsk-tsked, Gemma donned a shocked expression, though, in truth, neither lady had the least notion what Pam might be, for they played none of the card games enjoyed by fashionable ladies and gentlemen. Gemma chose to keep that information to herself, however, saying, "Sir, as you have denied us the joys of loo, we have but two other choices: Fox and Geese or draughts."

It spoke much for the gentleman's composure that he did not so much as blink at the naming of those two very childish games.

"Or," she added, hoping to goad him into showing his true colors, "we might beguile the hour with a round of Hunt-the-slipper or Blindman's Bluff. And let us not forget Hoop and Hide."

"What," he said, giving her a look that said he knew what she was about by proposing such infantile entertainment, "no Puss-in-the-corner?"

Gemma batted her eyelashes as she had seen Alicia do when trying to feign innocence. "Why, sir, I cannot credit that you would suggest such a game as that. Surely you must know that Puss-in-the-corner requires five players."

Whatever his reaction to her saucy teasing, it was lost forever, or so Gemma thought, for the maid chose that moment to announce that the nuncheon was served. Mr. Jamison was invited to join the family, and he readily accepted the invitation. It was when he stepped aside to allow Nora and Gemma to precede him from the room that he spoke. The words were little more than a whisper, and they were meant for Gemma's ears only.

"Minx," he said. "If you think I was deceived by that Cheltingham drama you enacted for my benefit, allow me to disabuse you of the misconception."

She batted her lashes again. "Drama? Why, sir, what *can* you mean?"

"You know," he said, and the light in his green eyes told her that he issued a new challenge—a challenge that had nothing whatever to do with the original one. "I give you fair warning, minx, mind how you toy with me, for when I play, I take no prisoners."

Chapter Six

"How is everyone at the manor?" Mrs. Nora Westin asked, availing herself of the crystal saltceller beside her plate.

Duncan had just cut into a tightly rolled veal collop, but he delayed tasting the lightly browned meat until he answered his hostess's question. "Everyone is well, ma'am. Including the newest addition to our party."

"A new edition? I had no idea the party had grown."

"It has, indeed, for my cousin, Mr. Nevil Montgomery, arrived unexpectedly Tuesday evening."

"What a delightful surprise," the lady said.

Because he could agree only that it was a surprise, with little of delight in it, Duncan made no reply; instead, he gave his attention once again to the savory collops.

The food was simple, yet well prepared, and though the small dining parlor, with its round oak table, was not to be compared with the spacious dining room at Howarth Manor, the meal and the company were far superior to anything Duncan had experienced for the past several days.

"What a coincidence," Miss Westin said, "that your relative should happen to be in the neighborhood. Was there a reason for his journey here?"

"I believe he said he was to meet a party of friends in Duddingham, and from there they were to continue together to some hunting box or other. Of course, when Mrs. Westin—Alicia, she asked us to call her, there being two Mrs. Westins—heard that Nevil was put up at the Blue Lion, she insisted that he remove to the manor without further delay."

"Another gentleman," the lady with the freckles muttered beneath her breath. "Dear Alicia must be overjoyed."

Meow! Duncan felt his lips twitch ever so slightly. It would appear there was a puss in the corner after all, and this one had claws. Considering discretion the better part of valor, he refrained from comment; instead, he chose to keep his eyes on his plate and his thoughts to himself.

It was Ceddy who broke the silence that followed Miss Gemma Westin's catty remark. "Is Mr. Nevil Montgomery related to me as well, Cousin?"

"In a manner of speaking. His relationship to you is on the same footing as mine. Sir Frederick is the link between us all, for he is brother to Nevil's father and to my mother."

"Shall I like my new cousin?"

"Ceddy!" his mother scolded. "Such a question is highly impolite."

Impolite or not, Duncan wished he could answer the query honestly. The boy would not like Nevil—not if the fellow revealed his true nature. Unfortunately, Nevil might choose to make himself agreeable, especially if he hoped to disarm Ceddy and those who would protect the boy from harm.

There! Duncan had finally let himself think the unthinkable: that his cousin had come to Suffolk for some nefarious purpose, and that he had reason to wish Ceddy ill.

Nevil's arrival in Duddingham on the very day of Ceddy's "accident" certainly gave rise to suspicion; especially if the fellow had somehow learned that Sir Frederick wished to adopt Ceddy and make him his heir.

But had Nevil discovered that piece of information? Had he been expecting to inherit Montgomery Park and the fortune that went with it?

A profligate and a gambler, Nevil was always in need of funds. If the need was pressing, if he was badly dipped, then the likelihood of his being named Sir Frederick's heir would be enough to quiet the majority of Nevil's creditors, as well as anyone who might be holding his gambling vowels. The expectation alone of such a fortune would allow Nevil to continue in his present mode of living.

The question remained, however, had Nevil's financial problems reached dire proportions—dire enough to threaten his self-indulgent way of life and his reputation with the ton? Was he desperate enough for funds to try to stop the adoption? Worse yet, was he wicked enough to injure a child?

Duncan did not know the answer to either question, but until he knew more, it behooved him to do what he could to make Ceddy safe from further "poachers." He thanked heaven for this nasty weather; at least it kept everyone indoors.

As if on cue, the lad said, "You should be able to see a bit of the countryside presently, Cousin, for Amos says the rain will end later this afternoon."

"And is Amos a diviner of such matters? Is he to be believed?"

The boy had just taken an overlarge bite of plum tart

swimming in clotted cream, so he contented himself with nodding his head.

"Amos has a sixth sense about the weather," Mrs. Westin explained. "That and finding lost items. We have learned to rely upon him for such things."

"He's the one to consult," Ceddy said, swallowing quickly, "when you want to have a bit of fun out-of-doors. You know the sort of thing I mean, Cousin—a day of boating and fishing, attending a fair, having a picnic—truly enjoyable pursuits."

The boy's face brightened suddenly. "Could we have a picnic, Mother? We have not had one in ever so long a time."

"It sounds a fine idea, Son."

"And may we do it like we used to, with lemonade and sandwiches in a basket? And some of Cook's special ginger-bread men?"

His mother raised her eyebrows in mock surprise. "Must you even ask? It would not be a picnic without the ginger-bread men."

"Famous!"

"I beg you, Ceddy," Miss Gemma Westin said, entering a caveat, "do not run immediately to the kitchen with your request for gingerbread. Let us delay the outing at least until such time as the lane has dried up a bit. Slogging through a quagmire is not my idea of a pleasure trip."

The boy had been too long restricted to the cottage, and he would hear no suggestion of waiting. "We need not use the lane, not if we go to the windmill like we used to. We can walk there."

"Walk?" the lady said. "Across all that boggy land? Why, before your mother and I had traveled half the distance, our hems would be soaked through and our boots caked with mud, and I daresay we would resemble nothing so much as a pair of Gypsies."

"You could wear pattens," Ceddy suggested.

"Pattens! You wish me to walk more than a mile with a pair of wooden overshoes lashed to my boots?" She lifted her eyes heavenward, as if seeking patience. "I thank you, Ceddy, but I believe I must decline that suggestion."

"But, Gemma," Ceddy continued, his expression resembling that of a puppy denied both love and sustenance, "only think how disappointed Cousin Duncan will be if he is obliged to leave the fens without seeing all the birds."

Gemma had just raised her glass to her lips, and she almost choked upon a sip of water. "Ceddy! There was no mention of . . . What I mean to say, I am persuaded Mr. Jamison would not care at all for the kind of rustic picnics we have."

The boy turned upon Duncan a look of such beseeching that only a conscienceless lout could have failed to be moved. "You would like to see the birds, would you not, sir?"

"I should like it very much, my boy."

"Famous!" Ceddy cried, his spirits miraculously restored. "I knew you would wish to go. What fun we shall have."

In his enthusiasm, the lad stuffed another large bite of tart in his mouth. Unfortunately, some of the clotted cream failed to make it inside, falling, instead, upon his chin.

"Ceddy!" his mother again scolded. "Mind your manners. You have cream on your face."

The boy wiped his chin with his napkin, but he was unrepentant. With an impish grin, he said, "Your pardon, Mother, I did not know that cream upon one's face was bad manners, especially since Gemma puts it on her freckles every night before she goes to bed."

"Ceddy!" both ladies yelled at once.

Gemma could not decide what she most wanted to do: cover her face with her napkin so she need never look at their guest again, or put her hands about Master Cedric Creighton's neck and wring it until he squawked like a chicken. How dare the boy reveal something so personal, and so embarrassing! Especially before a sophisticated man like Duncan Jamison.

When she steeled herself to glance in that gentleman's direction, what she saw only increased her chagrin, for his eyes were alight, and he was having trouble schooling his lips. It was obvious he wanted desperately to laugh, but somehow he managed to master the urge.

Finally, after several moments of strained silence, he said, "Ceddy, my boy, you should recommend to Miss Westin that she discontinue that particular regimen, for it is a waste of good cream. Depend upon it, cream only works on freckles."

"But, Cousin, Gemma *has* freckles."

"I believe you are mistaken there, lad, for those are not freckles." He looked directly at Gemma then, and his gaze captured hers, holding it by the sheer strength of his personality, blue eyes a captive to green. "No," he said softly, all signs of humor gone, "I am convinced that the charming sprinkle across your sister's nose is nothing less than angel kisses."

The next three hours were spent in the small parlor. An air of cheerful frivolity dominated the gathering, with neither acrostics nor hide-the-thimble beneath the dignity of the handsome gentleman from London. Due to the boisterousness of the games, the players were soon on a more relaxed footing, and in a very short time they had dropped all formality. There being too many ladies named Westin, first names soon became the order of the day.

Everyone was in good spirits; everyone, that is, except Gemma. For Gemma, who was still reeling from the information that the angels had kissed her nose, another blow was dealt her equilibrium when Ceddy challenged his teammate to a show of strength.

It was Jamison's fault, of course, for he happened to mention that Ceddy's father, Lieutenant Charles Creighton, had taught him to wrestle when they were youths. After Ceddy heard how it was done, using only the hand and forearm, nothing would do the boy but to have a go at it.

Naturally, Jamison accepted the challenge.

Because the two competitors required unrestricted movement of their arms and shoulders, the gentleman asked permission to remove his coat. Nora gave her consent without a second thought. It was when their guest removed the snug garment, with Ceddy acting as his valet, that Gemma was obliged to take a seat.

Without even realizing that she stared, she watched Jamison lay his coat across the back of the settee, then take his place at the work table. He retained his waistcoat, of course, but while he explained the rules of the contest to Ceddy, he unfastened the wristband of his white lawn shirt and began to roll up the right sleeve. Totally unaware of his audience, he did not stop until the roll was above his elbow, leaving his entire forearm bare.

With his arm exposed, Gemma was no longer in doubt as to why his hands had felt so strong upon her waist. The gentleman might be slender, but he was beautifully formed and marvelously fit. In fact, there appeared to be a muscle in the front as well as the back of his forearm, and as he showed Ceddy the requisite position to take prior to the contest, those amazing swells moved. Each time he contracted or relaxed his arm, the muscles would expand or relax as well, and the fluid rhythm of the movement did strange things to the rhythm of Gemma's heart.

She tried diverting her attention to his wrist, but as

a distraction that thick, powerful-looking joint proved a complete failure. Like his arm, Jamison's wrist was surprisingly tanned and lightly covered by fine, brown hair, and at the sight of it, Gemma felt the beating inside her chest accelerate to a virtual pounding.

Why no one noticed the noise, she could not say; she could only be grateful that the clamor went unremarked.

"We need a short stack of books, my boy, on which you may put your elbow, for our hands must be at the same height."

Three books were deemed appropriate, and once the opponents were seated opposite each other, their right palms placed together and their corresponding elbows set firmly upon table or books, the contest began. The battle did not last more than a few seconds, and even at that, it was obvious their guest was trying to delay the inevitable outcome to allow Ceddy a sense that he was truly competing.

"I could never best your father," he said once the boy's arm had been pushed down to the level of the books, "but I tried every time we met."

"You were never victorious?" Ceddy asked. "My father always won?"

"Always. Of course, as the years passed, Charles required more seconds in which to pin my arm to the table." He was silent for a moment. "Unfortunately, we never got to pit our skills against one another as grown men."

After Jamison unrolled his sleeve and fastened the wristband, he reached inside his watch pocket and extracted a handsome fob chain upon which was fastened a golden guinea. "Charles gave me this coin," he said.

The boy's eyes were big as buttons. "My father gave it to you?"

"He did, and I have a suggestion to make."

"What . . . what suggestion, Cousin?"

"I propose that we continue the contest your father and I never got to finish. Each time we meet," he said, "what say you to our having a go at it? I promise I shall never insult you by letting you win, and when, in some future year, you finally best me by pinning my arm to the table, I shall present you with this coin Charles gave to me."

"But . . . but what if we never meet again, Cousin?"

"Have no fear of that, my boy. We shall certainly meet again, and often."

Ceddy greeted the prospect with a sincere smile. "Famous, sir!"

Gemma's reaction to the promised encounters was far more complex, for while she delighted in Ceddy's new-found camaraderie with his cousin, she was suddenly reminded that Duncan Jamison had come into Suffolk not to meet Ceddy, but to assist his aunt and uncle in their plans to adopt the boy. If he expected to see the lad often, did he believe the plan was still in effect? She had thought everything was settled, for all three of the adults seemed to have accepted Nora's refusal to give up her son. As well, no pressure was being brought to bear upon the mother, and no overt gestures had been made to win over the boy's affections.

Before Gemma had an opportunity to put her thoughts in proper order, Amos presented himself in the arched doorway of the parlor. Across his arm was the rubberized coat, and in his hands he carried the gentleman's boots, now clean and mud free. "Rain's gone," he said, "and the sun'll be out anon."

"Ah, Amos," Mr. Jamison said, standing and reclaiming his coat from the chair, "your timing is perfect, for I must return to the manor house." To Ceddy he said, "Shall I tell our uncle that you were pleased with your telescope?"

"Oh, yes, sir. Tell him I like it of all things, and that I

hope he will show me a few of the particulars of its use when the lane is dry enough for him to come for tea.''

Gemma watched their guest don his snug coat and found the action very nearly as interesting as witnessing its removal. Though she knew she should have averted her eyes when he stepped into his boots and worked his feet inside the snug-fitting leather, she did not do so. Nor, when he caught her watching him, did she apologize for staring.

Their eyes met, and for a moment it seemed as if everyone else had disappeared, that they were the only two people in the world. When he continued to regard her, causing her breathing to slow almost to a stop, it was easy to push all other thoughts from her mind. After all, the subject of the adoption had not been mentioned again, and she had no reason to suspect that the matter was not settled.

Once Jamison was completely dressed, and looking every inch the London gentleman, he returned to the parlor and took his leave of Nora, bowing, then raising her fingertips to his lips. "Thank you, ma'am, for a wonderful day."

"Oh, no, sir. It is I who should thank you, for rescuing us from the doldrums."

He did not argue the point, but turned instead to Gemma. "Madam," he said, "I shall look forward to our picnic. With or without the pattens."

Before she could reply, he lifted her hand as he had done Nora's, his strong fingers holding hers gently. "Until then," he said, then he bent and touched his firm lips to her skin, lingering a moment or two longer than he had when bidding Nora farewell.

At the feel of his lips, every nerve in Gemma's flesh seemed to react, causing a tingling sensation to course up her arm. Taken aback by that unexpected tingle, and by the warmth his touch ignited inside her, she eased her hand from his. Not wanting him to know of her reaction, she managed somehow to exhibit a calm she was far from feeling. "Good day to you, sir."

She waited until she heard his footfalls upon the flagstone path, then she excused herself to Nora and ran up the stairs. Only when she reached the privacy of her bedchamber did she allow herself the freedom to react. After a sharply exhaled breath, she murmured a faint, "Oh, my," then she hurried to the window where she could watch Duncan Jamison as he passed the mounting block and the service tree. All too quickly, his long, purposeful strides took him from her sight.

When he was gone, she sighed, though she called herself a fool for having done so. It was but a kiss on the hand. The kind of kiss such a man as he must bestow upon hostesses—young or old, handsome or homely—from one end of London to the other. "Of a certainty," she said aloud, "the salute will have meant nothing to him, and only a foolish country miss like me would give it the least significance."

And yet, when she caught her reflection in the glass of the windowpane, her fingertips moved of their own accord to the pale freckles across her nose. Nothing less than angel kisses, he had called them. She sighed again, but this time she let herself enjoy the memory. Duncan Jamison may have kissed the hands of hundreds of London hostesses, but surely he had never told even one of those ladies that her face had been kissed by the angels.

Duncan covered the distance between the cottage and the manor house carriageway in something less than half an hour, and though the sun had, indeed, come out, he could still hear the occasional sound of captured raindrops falling from the leaves of the trees. As he reached the wrought-iron gates and turned left, he heard something else, the crunch of boots upon the gravel carriageway. The man who strolled toward him was Nevil Montgomery, and for the moment he was unaware of Duncan's presence.

"Your face is pensive," Duncan said by way of greeting, "as though you are deep in thought."

Nevil looked up quickly, a flash of annoyance in his eyes, though the emotion was immediately masked by a practiced smile. "In truth, Jamison, you see me not so much in thought as in search of a bit of quiet."

"Do not let me interrupt you, then."

"No, no. You misread my purpose." Turning, he matched his step to Duncan's and the two of them strolled toward the manor. "It was only from our toadying host that I wished to escape."

"You find Mr. Titus Westin's company displeasing, do you?"

"Displeasing?" Nevil looked down his slender nose. "More to the point, I find the fellow officious in the extreme, scarcely less so than his butler. Actually, 'tis little to distinguish between the two men, and I begin to suspect that both are descended from a long line of shopkeepers."

"You are very censuring. I should think a man such as you—one who spends much of his time in other men's houses—would be a bit more charitable in his assessment of those whose hospitality he enjoys."

Though Nevil's countenance remained unchanged, his hands curled into fists. "What would you know of the matter? How could a man such as *you*—one who enjoys the benefits of a promised inheritance complete with a prosperous estate and a stately home—possibly understand? Believe me, when a gentleman is fated to spend his life as a guest in other men's establishments, 'tis difficult not to compare the merits of those who have with the merits of those who have not. Furthermore, 'tis impossible

not to feel displeasure when it is obvious that those who
have are undeserving of their fate.''

"And what, I wonder, entitles you to be the judge?''

Mr. Nevil Montgomery turned upon Duncan a look that
was as angry as it was quickly banished. "What is my entitle-
ment? Surely my status as one of the have nots bestows
upon me the right to be arbiter." He laughed, but the
sound had no humor in it. " 'Tis my right to frown upon
the wealthy, dear boy. My joy to make sport of them. My
one amusement to ridicule them at my leisure.''

To Duncan's relief, this revealing display was cut short
by their arrival at the moat, a circumstance that put him
in mind of something from the Bible regarding motes of
another kind and judging others as one would wish to be
judged. If Gemma Westin's suitor, the curate, were here, he
could probably quote both chapter and verse. All Duncan
knew for certain was that Nevil Montgomery was a very
bitter man; moreover, one who harbored a deep sense of ill
use. Jealousy had made Nevil angry. Angry and dangerous.

This new view of his cousin supported Duncan's suspicion that Nevil was somehow connected with the shooting
of Ceddy Creighton, and he determined to be watchful,
both of the boy and of Nevil. Knowing he could not be
in two places at once, he determined to write a letter
immediately once he reached his bedchamber—a letter
beseeching assistance. The question of who he would ask
for such help did not arise, for whenever Duncan was in
need of a friend, the name of only one man entered his
mind.

Chapter Seven

Friday and Saturday were as beautiful as Amos had fore-told, and, as a result, Sunday was everything a picnicker could want. The sun put on a show fit for a king, and any dampness that may have survived the warmth of the previous two days soon evaporated. As a result, the roads were usable once again, and the inhabitants of both the manor house and Howarth Cottage attended morning wor-ship services at the village church.

All the inhabitants, that is, except for Nora, who awoke with the headache, an occurrence so unheard of that Gemma immediately offered to remain at home to attend her. "I should have guessed you were ill, for you seem restless. As well, while we were at table, you scarcely touched your breakfast."

Gemma had been about to don her bonnet when Nora knocked at her bedchamber door, but now she set the pretty chip straw on the bed beside her gloves and reticule. "I shall send Amos to the manor immediately to tell them that we will not be needing the landau this morning."

"What nonsense, my love. I would not think of your staying home. Especially not when you have chosen to wear one of your new frocks." She regarded the simple, high-waisted confection. "That lavender-blue muslin was an inspired choice, by the way. It is vastly becoming to you."

"I know what you are about, Nora, and I will not be distracted by compliments. If you are unwell, you should not be left alone."

"I am not unwell. And now I wish I had not mentioned it, for it is the merest trifle, I assure you."

Gemma appeared not to have heard her. "I know the very thing to bring you around. What say you to a nice cup of tea? I shall put a bit of honey in it, the way you like it." Not waiting long enough for a reply, she was halfway to the stairs before Nora could stay her hurried steps.

"Gemma!"

When Gemma stopped, her eyes wide with surprise, Nora moderated her tone. "Thank you, my love, but I do not want tea, with or without honey. And I definitely do not wish to be treated like an invalid. If you would please me, put on that pretty new bonnet and go down to the mounting block where Ceddy is waiting for you. I believe I hear the horses now."

"But—"

"No buts. In all likelihood, what I need is another hour upon my bed, after which I shall be right as a trivet."

Gemma looked as though she might argue, but she must have thought better of it, for after a moment, she returned to her bedchamber and set the bonnet on her head. Taking up her gloves and reticule, she paused in the corridor only long enough to kiss Nora's cheek, then she descended the stairs and quit the cottage.

Though Nora felt like the grouchiest, most unappreciative creature in nature, when she went to the window in Gemma's bedchamber where she could see the lane, she was happy to be alone at last. She had no idea what was bothering her, making her so out of sorts, but whatever it was, she was convinced that listening to one of Mr. Bascombe Newley's interminable sermons would not improve her disposition.

She had been correct in her statement to Gemma; she had, indeed, heard horses. The first team to pass pulled Sir Frederick's handsome maroon chaise, and following close behind the chaise was a showy chestnut—obviously a new horse—that was hitched between the shafts of the pretty yellow-trimmed cabriolet Philip Westin had purchased just before his illness.

Nora did not see the face of the gentleman who handled the chestnut's ribbons, though judging by the York tan coat that fit his slender figure to perfection, he definitely was not Titus. There was no mistaking his companion. It was Alicia, and by the laughter that disturbed the peace of the morning, she was quite happy to be in company with the stranger.

Never reserved in her dress, today Alicia had outdone herself by choosing to wear a Dutch-pink pelisse and a matching high-crowned silk bonnet, a bonnet whose poke was adorned with at least two dozen grebe feathers dyed a most unnatural pink. As the cabriolet whizzed on by, Nora shook her head in amazement at the woman's ensemble.

Last came the antiquated landau, a conveyance Philip had ceased to use several years back when the duel hoods had begun to leak. Though the stables at the manor house contained a well-sprung barouche, Alicia had deemed the landau a suitable conveyance for the inhabitants of the cottage; therefore, each Sunday it was their transportation to town. At least the horses were reliable, having been acquired by Nora's late husband. The groom brought the pair to a halt beside the mounting block, and when Gemma and Ceddy climbed aboard the old carriage, it creaked in protest at even their negligible weight.

Nora remained at the window until the carriage was out of sight and the lane was once again quiet, then she returned to her own room. Instead of seeking her bed, however, she decided that fresh air would be of more benefit than sleep. She did not suffer from the headache. She never had. She had claimed it because it was an acceptable complaint, and because the malady that really plagued her was much too personal to name. If it had a name.

All she knew was that for some time now she had felt a sort of wistfulness, a longing that would not go away. She yearned for something, yet she knew not what. It was not—could not be—loneliness, for she had Ceddy, a son any mother would cherish, and she had Gemma, who was both sister and friend to her. Still, there was something missing in her life, a vague something she dared not admit, even to herself.

Hoping if she did not dwell upon her restlessness it might disappear, she donned the much-washed blue muslin dress she wore when gardening, defiantly leaving off her stays. While she brushed through her thick curls, letting them fall as they would about her shoulders and back, she found the idea of forcing her hair into a suitable knot, or confining it beneath a cap, almost more than she could endure. Having already dispensed with her restrictive undergarments, she decided to leave her hair free as well, and using a blue satin ribbon she discovered among the notions in her sewing box, she tied her blond tresses loosely at the nape of her neck.

Dressed as she was, she felt better, almost defiant, and as free as a schoolgirl. If she were not a woman on the verge of her thirty-fourth birthday, and if she were not a widow twice over, she might have strolled along the lane, listening to a party of sedge warblers mimicking the sparrows. She might even have gone to the river, cast off her shoes, and wiggled her bare toes in the sun-warmed water.

She did neither of those things, of course. After sighing at the unsuitability of her errant thoughts, she pulled on an apron, found her trowel and hand spade, then went out to the wildflower garden, her purpose to uproot the weeds that seemed unwilling to understand that, like her, they, too, must be subdued.

The sun felt wonderful upon her back, and after several minutes of kneeling beside a bed of yellow flag iris, she sat back on her heels, closed her eyes, and let the warmth have its way with her face. How long she remained thus, she could not say, but suddenly, without having heard a sound, she knew that someone was watching her. Instantly, she opened her eyes.

A man stood on the flagstone path, not thirty feet away from her. Why he was there, or how he had come upon her so quietly, she had no idea, but even though she was alone at the cottage, she was not afraid.

"You should wear a hat," he said softly. "Did no one ever tell you what the sun will do to smooth, lovely skin?"

Nora knew she should tell the man to be on his way, or at the very least she should give him a set down for speaking so impertinently, yet she did neither of those things. She kept her peace. It seemed a hundred years since anyone had even looked at her complexion, and she was disinclined to speak sharply to someone who had not only looked but also declared it to be lovely.

Besides, why should she treat him rudely? He was bothering no one. If the truth be known, she rather liked the look of him, for laugh lines crinkled at the corners of the brownest eyes she had ever seen. As well, his voice was low and soothing, and though he was not dressed in the height of fashion, neither was he clad as a Gypsy.

"I do not wish to wear a hat," she said. "At least, not today."

"Is there something special about today?"

"No. Yes." She shook her head. "Perhaps."

He chuckled, and it seemed to Nora that she had never heard a more natural sound. It was unpretentious, and honest as the song of the sedge warblers.

"Who are you?" she asked quietly.

The question had come unbidden, for she had not been the least bit curious to know his name, not so far. She should, of course, have been curious as well as frightened, for he was a stranger, and decidedly brawny. There was no other word to describe a man with such broad shoulders and such large, competent-looking hands. Furthermore, even though his manners were easy and his disposition seemed happy, there was an undeniable something in his bearing that warned the world, here was a man best left unchallenged.

"My name is Yarborough. Steven Yarborough."

"Steven Yarborough," she said, testing the name upon her tongue. "My name is—"

"Lorelei."

He spoke the word so softly she could not be certain if he had actually said it, or if she had only imagined it. "What did you call me?"

"Lorelei," he said again. "I did not believe you existed. Yet here you are."

He smiled then, as if the joke was on him. "My father was a sailor, and he used to tell me stories about *Die Lorelei*. Tales of the hauntingly beautiful siren with the golden curls and eyes the color of the ocean waves."

"What did she do?" Nora asked a bit breathlessly.

"The Lorelei suns herself upon the rock, awaiting the arrival of the ships, then she uses her beauty to mesmerize the sailors, luring them to their fate."

Nora found she could not take her gaze from those dark-brown orbs. If there was any mesmerizing going on here, she had a pretty fair notion who was doing it.

"I am Nora Westin," she said quickly, hoping the words would break the spell he had cast.

It worked. When she said her name, the stranger removed his broad-brimmed hat and made her a bow, and the commonplace gesture seemed to free her from her fanciful thoughts.

With his head bared, she could see him better. He was not handsome in the truest sense, yet there was something compellingly male about the hardness of his jaw and the slight shadow upon cheeks shaved probably as recently as that morning. His hair, like his eyebrows, was thick and black, and worn a bit longer than was stylish. Though he was probably no more than thirty-five, the sun glinted off a smattering of gray at his temples.

He stood very still, as if allowing her to look her fill, and when Nora realized what she had been doing, and that he was aware as well, she looked away. Trying to ignore the accelerated beating of her heart, she gave her attention to the trowel she still held.

"So, Miss Nora," he said, "do you work here?"

"I live here, Mr. Yarborough. And it is not *Miss*, but *Mrs.*"

Long after the stranger had tipped his hat and quit the garden, Nora remained, though any thoughts of attacking weeds had vanished from her mind. She merely sat there, pleased to be in the open air, and never once did she wonder what had become of the wistfulness that had plagued her earlier, or why the day suddenly seemed so filled with promise.

While Nora recalled every word the stranger had said, marveling that one man could be such a fascinating conversationalist, three miles away, in Duddingham, the parishioners of the handsome old Norman church filed out into the churchyard, their eyes dulled by the inane sermon they had just endured.

Master Cedric Creighton, unhampered by the constraints of adulthood, was one of the first somnambulants to exit the hallowed edifice, and when Duncan finally stepped out into the sunshine, he spied Ceddy standing some distance away.

"Is this to be our picnic day?" he asked, coming up behind the lad.

"Sir!" A ready smile lit the boy's face. "How glad I am to see you, for I was not certain you would remember your promise."

He ruffled the boy's dark-blond hair. "Never fear, lad, for I have the memory of . . . of . . . well, I forget the name of the animal, but I—"

"Cousin!" Ceddy said, laughing at the jest. "You are the most complete hand."

"That he is," Nevil said, joining them as though he had been invited to do so. "And you, bantling, must be my young cousin."

Still smiling, Ceddy replied, "I am, sir, if you are Mr. Nevil Montgomery. How do you do? I am pleased to make your acquaintance at last."

"Upon my word," Nevil said, raising his quizzing glass to his eye and staring at Ceddy, "what have we here? A youngster possessed of both looks and manners? I daresay our esteemed uncle was pleased to make *your* acquaintance."

At the newcomer's patronizing tone, the smile faded from Ceddy's lips. "As to that, sir, I cannot say. I know only that I was happy to meet him."

"The pleasure was entirely mine," Sir Frederick said, approaching them with Lady Montgomery on one arm and Mrs. Alicia Westin on the other, the bright pink grebe feathers on her bonnet rising and settling with each step she took. "When his aunt and I were finally able to call in at the cottage yesterday, we could not have been happier at the way the boy has grown since last we saw him. Could we, my dear?"

Lady Montgomery made no reply; however, since she was at that moment touching her gloved hand to Ceddy's cheek and smiling at him in a way that quite put the boy to the blush, no answer was necessary.

Realizing that Ceddy was in good hands with his aunt and uncle nearby, Duncan looked around to see what had become of the ladies from the cottage. He spied Gemma immediately, for she was being detained on the church porch by her Bible-quoting admirer. The curate held her hand firmly between both of his, obliging her to remain where she stood or else make a scene.

Because Newley's sermon had been like the man himself—filled with sound but no substance—Duncan had merely nodded at the end of the service and left the church. Now, however, with the parson possessing himself overlong of Gemma's hand, Duncan saw that a meeting between them was inevitable.

"My stepmother was a victim to the headache this morning," Gemma said, trying to slip her hand free of Newley's grasp, "and because she was unable to leave her bed, I feel I must return to her as quickly as possible, to offer what support I may."

"My dear Miss Westin," the curate said, still not releasing her, "your devotion to Mrs. Westin does you credit. As we are told in Leviticus, chapter 27, verse 28, 'Every devoted thing is most holy unto—' "

"Good morning," Duncan said, drawing near the porch. The curate was less pleased than he might have been by a greeting from a visitor to the parish, but for her part, Gemma was grateful for the interruption.

"Jamison," she said, "a lovely day, is it not?"

"Quite," he said.

Gemma breathed a sigh of relief when Jamison did not walk on by, but stepped up onto the porch. Standing beside Mr. Newley, he grasped the curate's wrist as though wanting to shake the man's hand, and because the barrister was several inches taller than Mr. Newley, only a very little pressure was required before Gemma was released.

Obviously not wanting to make a scene himself, Jamison shook the younger man's hand briefly, then he took Gemma by the elbow and led her away at a brisk pace. "My aunt has bid me bring you to her, ma'am. She is desirous of ascertaining some information that only you can supply."

"Certainly, sir. I shall be most happy to give Lady Montgomery whatever assistance is within my power."

Once they were out of the parson's hearing, Mr. Jamison slowed his step, then he said rather offhandedly, "We need not hurry. Actually, I am not at all certain that Aunt Evelyn will recall which piece of information she sought. Perhaps we should forget the matter entirely."

"Forget about it? I cannot do that, for surely her ladyship will be expecting me to . . ."

Gemma looked up into his face, and though his countenance was one of studied innocence, the light in his eyes betrayed him. "Sir! Never tell me that you fabricated that story just to secure my willingness to come away with you?"

"Pray inform me, madam, how else I was to accomplish the feat? Having failed to set to memory any applicable Scripture, I had no choice but to, er, make use of my fertile imagination."

"In other words, you told a falsehood."

"Falsehood! Madam, I am heartily offended. We of the

legal profession prefer to call it a judicious rearrangement of the facts."

"You would do," she said.

"Of course we would," he replied affably.

Gemma would not let herself laugh. "Sir, if I may be allowed to paraphrase Mr. Shakespeare, a falsehood by any other name would still smell like a barefaced lie."

"Mere semantics," he replied, apparently not at all offended by her plain speaking. "Let us but look at the facts."

"You refer, of course, to the *rearranged* fact."

"Clever girl! I knew you would soon get the gist of the idea. Now, I will be happy to demonstrate the logic, should you wish to incorporate the system into your daily life."

Gemma was sorely tried in her efforts to keep a straight face. "I said nothing, sir, of adopting your lawyer's tricks."

"Of course not, for you have not yet seen how well they work. For example, my original statement—"

"The original 'falsehood,' " she said, as if to clarify the basis upon which they began.

He disregarded the interruption. "My original statement was that my aunt had bid me bring you to her for the purpose of asking you a question. Now, let us make a judicious rearrangement of the facts. Fact number one, my aunt is an educated woman, one who enjoys learning new things. Fact number two, who is to say that she does not wish to ask you any number of questions? Fact number three, if you were asked some particular question, I am persuaded you would prove knowledgeable on the subject."

"Yes, but—"

"All those statements are true, ergo, my original statement must also be true."

"But you failed to address that part of the original statement in which your aunt was said to have 'bid' you bring me to her.''

"Oh, well," he said, waving the matter away as though it was of little significance, "I made no mention of that part, because it was so obvious as to be self-explanatory."

"It is not obvious to me."

"If that is true, then Howarth Cottage must not number among its furnishings a looking glass."

"Sir?"

"You obviously have not seen yourself," he said softly.

He looked down at her then, and his gaze slowly traveled the contours of her jawline, lingering for several moments on her mouth, then settling upon her eyes. "Allow me to inform you, madam, that the lavender-blue of your frock has turned your eyes the color of early spring violets."

Spring violets? Rendered speechless by the compliment, Gemma could only stare.

"Seeing you thus," he continued, "with your eyes all velvety soft and the blue tinged with lilac, anyone would bid me bring you to them."

"Sir, I—"

"Jamison," Alicia called to him, causing several of the curious parishioners to turn and stare. "Yoo-hoo."

"There is the proof," Duncan said, looking down at Gemma. "I am being bid to bring you over now."

Gemma made a sound that bore an unfortunate resemblance to a snort. "By Alicia? A groat will net you a shilling she has not even noticed that I am with you."

"Jamison!" Alicia called again. "Do come here, for you must support me in my dispute with your cousin."

"Certainly," he replied. "What has the young rascal been saying?"

Alicia lifted her nose as though the breeze carried some unpleasant odor. "Children should be seen and not heard.

I referred not to the boy but to your other cousin, Mr. Nevil Montgomery.''

"I fear, ma'am," Duncan said, "that if you would seek an ally in that particular dispute, you must look otherwhere. Nevil and I gave up fighting with one another years ago."

"Yes," Nevil added. "Now we are the best of friends. Is that not so, Jamison?"

After hesitating for a matter of seconds, Jamison inclined his head politely. "There can be but one opinion on the subject."

The time for the picnic was set for two o'clock, and since Duncan was as unwilling as Gemma to see the ladies resort to pattens, he made it a point to stop in at the manor's handsome, brick-floored stables to discover from the head groom if the ladies of Howarth Cottage rode.

"Oh, yes, sir," the grizzled old fellow replied. He pointed to a shiny black mare with a white blaze on her forehead. "The mare over there were always Mrs. Westin's choice. Mrs. Philip Westin, I should say."

"A handsome animal."

"Right you are, sir. And as unfretful a mount as any lady could want. The mare'll give you no trouble, sir."

"What of Miss Westin? Do you recall if she had a favorite?"

The servant indicated a pretty white-maned sorrel filly who pranced around in her stall as if eager to be out-of-doors. Lowering his voice confidentially, the groom said, "She's called Lady's Pride, but best keep an eye on her, sir. She's frisky like, and Miss Gemma enjoys a good gallop."

"I take your meaning." Glancing down the length of the long building, Duncan asked if there was not something Ceddy could ride.

The groom looked toward the stall that held the showy chestnut used for the cabriolet; the animal had just been rubbed down and was now sipping water from a bucket held by an under-groom in a leather apron. "Master Ceddy was used to have a pony, sir. A sweet-tempered little Shetland."

"The very thing. Where is the creature now?"

Withdrawing a crumpled kerchief from his back pocket, the groom used it to wipe a spot from his hand, giving the task his full attention. "When the new master purchased that chestnut, he said we needed the stall. The pony were sold a fortnight back."

Dismayed by the thoughtlessness of such an act, coming as it did so close upon the boy's loss of his home, Duncan was obliged to remind himself that he was a guest in Titus Westin's house. Westin was the legally entitled master of the house, and as such he had a right to sell or keep his cattle as he saw fit. It was an undeniable truth, and knowing this enabled Duncan to speak politely several minutes later when he found his host ensconced in an overstuffed chair in the bookroom, a plate of sandwiches and a bottle of port on the table at his elbow.

"The ladies of Howarth Cottage have planned a picnic, sir, to which they have graciously invited me. Since their destination is the fen windmill, a place unreachable by carriage, I was wondering, Mr. Westin, if you would object to having the ladies' preferred mounts sent to them for the afternoon?"

Titus readily agreed, apparently happy that he had not been asked to do anything that would necessitate his bestirring himself. "Happy to oblige, Jamison. The groom will know which of the cattle to prepare."

So it was that an hour later, when Duncan halted Aries at the mounting block, he found the under-groom there before him, holding a bridle in each hand, one for the mare, the other for the restive filly. Nodding to the man, Duncan dismounted and looped the bay's reins over a limb of the service tree.

When he would have gone to the door of the cottage to fetch the ladies, he heard them coming, for they chattered happily, apparently as eager as the filly to be on their way. Nora was first on the flagstone path, and as she walked, the faille of her sage-green habit whooshed against the tops of her riding boots. As usual, her dark-blond curls had already begun to slip from beneath her hat, but she was a pretty sight for all that.

"Good afternoon, ma'am," he greeted. "I trust your headache is gone."

Though the lady blushed as if she were guilty of something, she bestowed upon him one of her sweet smiles. "Thank you, sir, I feel wonderful. It was considerate of you to think of the horses."

"Very," Gemma added, "and I, for one, am ready for a good gallop."

Duncan was on the verge of giving the young lady a warning about not exceeding her abilities when he caught sight of her—caught sight and immediately forget everything he had meant to say.

She wore a simple, smoke-gray habit fashioned of poplin, and though her ensemble was a far cry from the fashionable costumes worn by the ladies he usually escorted, the effect of the gray upon Miss Gemma Westin's blue eyes and sun-streaked blond hair left him wondering why he had ever thought the girl merely pretty. She was lovely, and as refreshing as a cool drink after a long ride.

Ceddy brought up the rear, and though his right arm no longer rested in the sling, the bulk beneath his shirt indicated that his shoulder was still bound. "Shall I walk?" he asked shyly, forcing Duncan's thoughts back to the moment.

"Only if that is your wish, scamp." Not for the world would Duncan have disclosed the fate of the lad's pony. "I had thought you and I might ride double. That way, you can tell me the proper route."

The boy brightened immediately. "The very thing, Cousin. I should have thought of that myself."

Nora chose to use the mounting block, but Gemma allowed Duncan to toss her into the saddle. When they were set, Duncan remounted Aries and held him steady while the under-groom gave Ceddy a leg up behind the gelding.

"Ready, Amos?" the lad yelled.

Immediately, everyone looked back up the path, where Amos Littlejohn stood beside the rose arbor, a wicker basket over his arm. The giant wore an intense expression upon his homely face, but at a signal from Nora, the expression vanished and he took off at a run around the side of the house.

"There goes our food," Ceddy said. "Please, Cousin, may we start now?"

"Are you that hungry, my boy?"

Nora answered the question. "Ceddy is always hungry, but in this instance, he made a wager with Amos that he could not beat us to the windmill."

"I see. How much did you wager?"

"Tuppence, Cousin, but it is not the money. It is Amos. He runs so fast he always beats me."

"Then let us delay no longer. Perhaps we can put a winning mark in your column." Having ranged himself on the boy's side, he prodded the gelding with the heels of his boots, and they were on their way.

As it transpired, they did not outrun Amos Littlejohn. When they arrived at the end of the narrow wooded trail some twenty minutes later and reined in beside the seventeenth-century windmill, the servant was there before them, the glow of triumph on his face. He stood in the shade of a lone alder tree, leaning nonchalantly against the dark gray-brown bark as if he had been there for hours, and though his breathing was unlabored, his orange hair stuck out from his head much as the wind-turned blades protruded from the wheel set atop the oak tower of the windmill.

"I told you, Master Ceddy."

The lad muttered some young-boy expletive before sliding off the gelding, and though Duncan supposed he must have given him a hand down, he was unaware that he had done so, unaware of anything but the land before him. This was Duncan's first visit to the fens, and he had eyes for nothing but his surroundings. Beholding Duddingham Fen, he forgot all else in his awe of the unspoiled marsh-lands—land so wild, so untouched as to be practically primordial.

"Well, sir," Gemma said, reining in the sorrel beside the gelding, "what think you of our little Eden?"

"I think, madam, that the biblical garden could not have been so unlike this beautiful spot."

Duncan had never seen anything like it, for the fen was a seemingly endless stretch, a lush haven of green vegetation and brackish dark-blue water, where rich scrub and stands of tall herbs grew in abundance. The colors were unbelievable, for he spied meadowsweet and wild angelica growing beside pink-flowering agrimony hemp and yellow loosestrife, and no matter where he looked, butterflies of every hue and marking flitted from flower to flower. Meanwhile, birds beyond description took wing or alit, some remaining upon the land, others wading in the shallow water.

Lapwings, yellow wagtails, and blue-black buntings

searched at their leisure among the bullrushes and beds of reed and sedge that fringed the long stretches of pools and ditches. At the same time, the majestic osprey and the long-legged purple heron traveled the waters, partaking of nature's bounty, catching and eating their fill of fish, seemingly without a sense of hurry.

The stillness was disturbed only by the varied calls of the birds, the deep croaking of unseen frogs, and the occasional splash of a fish in the water, and while Duncan looked about him silently, Gemma chuckled. "A lawyer with nothing to say? I believe I must record this in my journal, for surely it is a rarity worth chronicling."

"Tease me if you will, madam, but what can one say when confronted by so much splendor? I had gained the impression that such places no longer existed."

The smile on Miss Gemma Westin's face vanished. "You were not mistaken, for the fens of East Anglia are disappearing at an alarming rate, drained by the great landowners so that more and more land might be used for cash crops."

Duncan could not stop himself from glancing at the windmill. The lady's father had been one of those landowners. Had Philip Westin been so innocent of greed that his daughter could now censure her neighbors? It was all well and good to point an accusing finger now that she was among the "have nots," but had she been similarly vocal when she lived in the manor house and shared in the added wealth from the crops?

"Was this not once your father's land?" he asked. "Did he not use that windmill over there to pump the water out?"

Gemma stiffened, quick to perceive the rationale behind his comments. "Do not be so ready to judge, sir. My grandfather, like his contemporaries, drained the land as fast as possible, drained it without once considering the peasants whose very livelihoods depended upon the reeds, the fish, and the wildlife of the fens.''

She lifted her chin defiantly. "But not so my father.''

Raising her arm, she made a sweeping gesture as if to call Duncan's attention to the expanse of beauty. "This marvelous place you see before you was almost completely drained when my father inherited the estate. This fen, and its reclamation, are due entirely to his efforts. If it were not for Philip Westin, Duddingham Fen would now be nothing but acres of flat, treeless farm land.''

She drew a deep, angry breath. "Furthermore, sir, allow me to inform you that the windmill you pointed to with such righteous disdain does not drain the fen. On the contrary, it pumps water back into it, helping the marsh-land rejuvenate itself, thereby offering sanctuary to who-knows-how-many species of birds, butterflies, and other wildlife.''

Duncan was not a little taken aback by her fervor. And more than a little embarrassed by his own unfounded conclusions. He was not usually so quick to judge others. If he kept this up, that sanctimonious curate would be quoting to him about the error of casting out the mote in one's broth-er's eye while ignoring the beam in one's own.

And rightly so!

"Your pardon, madam, I see I was inexcusably hasty with my judgment. Your father performed an admirable, and, I might add, an unselfish act, and I honor him for it. The past century saw the total depletion of many of the country's forests, and I fear it is the generations of the future who will feel the loss. Let us hope the generations of birds and animals to come will always find a home at Duddingham Fen.''

"May it be so," she said quietly. "To that end, I pray that Titus remains the indolent man he is."

"Why so? Do you have reason to believe he wishes to drain the fen?"

She shrugged her shoulders. "I sincerely hope not. The estate, including the fen, is his alone, and there is nothing that can be done to stop him doing whatever he wishes with it."

They were silent for a time, each lost in private thought, staring out across the shallow waters. It was some minutes later when Duncan felt her looking at him, and when he turned to her, a slow smile pulled at the corners of her mouth. "Sir Frederick informed us that you mean to stand for Parliament in the next election."

"That is my plan."

"Good. When you become the honorable member from your district, perhaps you can introduce legislation to stop the senseless destruction of our forests and the draining of the fens."

"*If* I become the honorable member from my district."

Her smile gave way to a chuckle. "If? This from the man who will not let a challenge go unanswered?"

Duncan allowed her to tease him. In fact, he rather enjoyed her playfulness. Most of the females of his acquaintance were disposed to flatter him or defer to his opinions; not so Miss Gemma Westin. But then, Gemma was not most females. She was an original; a lady with hitherto unknown depths.

In fact, if she had been a lad, he would have said she had pluck. Without a doubt she possessed a sort of gallantry. Not once during their acquaintance had he heard her bemoan the straitened circumstances of her life since her father's death, and though Gemma had been reared in the luxury of a large house, with a staff of servants to do her bidding, she never complained of the cramped quarters or her new, less than elegant surroundings.

Yes, she was an original. Not unlike the glorious fen itself, she was complex, colorful, and filled with the warmth of the sun.

"Sir," she said, "if you continue to look at me in that manner, I shall begin to suspect that I have a smut upon my face."

"No, madam, no smuts. Just the usual angel kisses."

He had said those words to her before, but for some reason, this time she blushed to the roots of her hair. As well, she lowered her eyelids, as if not wanting him to read her thoughts. Her lashes were pale, yet quite long, and he could not help noticing how softly they rested against her pink cheeks.

Of its own accord, his gaze slipped from her eyelashes to her full lips, lips as smooth and tempting as fresh-picked berries. In that moment Duncan knew an almost overwhelming desire to lean over and taste the sweetness.

He had decided to try his luck when Gemma suddenly lifted her lashes. Their gazes met and held, and when he leaned toward her, moving slowly so he would not take her unawares, she did not back away.

Unfortunately, though the young lady appeared willing, Lady's Pride took instant exception to Duncan's nearness and began tossing her head about, her white mane fanning the air. When the sorrel blew through her nose and began pawing the ground, she spooked the gelding as well, causing the larger animal to sidestep and snort his disapproval of such missishness.

"Easy, boy," Duncan cooed, patting Aries' neck. He was still trying to bring the horse under control when Gemma, having backed the filly out of harm's way, called out to him.

"Jamison," she said, a taunting quality in her voice, "do you dare circle the fen? This filly needs a good run."

Duncan was not certain to which filly she referred, Lady's Pride or herself, but even before he could accept the challenge, Gemma had turned the sorrel and galloped away. Naturally, he gave chase.

Chapter Eight

"The filly is far too frisky," Nora said. She did not address her remark to Gemma, but to Jamison, who sat beside Ceddy on the far side of the blanket. Having eaten her fill of the picnic sandwiches, she pressed her napkin to her lips, then set the linen on the blanket beside her. "I fear the animal will do herself, or Gemma, a harm."

"I wish you would not worry," Gemma said, "for Lady's Pride is actually quite sweet-tempered. She just needed some exercise. Any creature will grow restive if obliged to remain inactive overlong."

She pointed to an area not far removed from the picnic site where the sorrel, the mare, and the gelding were tethered, all three animals calmly munching grass, obviously in good accord with one another. "See for yourself. Now that she has had a good run, Lady's Pride is as docile as a lamb."

Gemma busied herself with selecting a gingerbread man from the half dozen that remained on a pewter tray in the middle of the blanket. She was no longer hungry, but choosing one of the dark-brown cakes served to keep Nora from looking into her eyes and possibly reading her thoughts.

The mare had not been the only creature in want of a good run. Gemma had needed one as well. When she and Duncan Jamison had locked gazes, something had passed between them, something that made her heart skip several beats, and Gemma had needed to get away from the man before she betrayed her growing feelings for him.

She had come close to letting him kiss her. *Letting him!* There was self-deception indeed, for if the truth be known, she had felt her lips purse in anticipation, and the mere recollection of her unseemly eagerness caused heat to surge through her entire body.

She had seen the way he was looking at her, and when she lowered her eyelashes, she had felt his continued scrutiny. Looking up had been a mistake, for though she had never been kissed, some female instinct told her what lay behind his darkening green eyes. He wanted to kiss her.

At the promise of the shared intimacy, she knew a growing excitement, for she very much wanted to feel Duncan Jamison's lips upon hers. He was tall and handsome, and so very charming, just such a man as she had always dreamed would one day take her in his arms and press—

"Snake!" Ceddy yelled, jumping up excitedly and breaking into Gemma's thoughts with the one word guaranteed to put all else from her mind.

"See it there?" he said, pointing to a spot some dozen feet from where they sat. "There it goes. See it winding its way toward that fen carr?"

Nora and Gemma both gasped, then they turned to watch in horror as Ceddy pursued the reptile toward the stand of alder trees.

"Do not be alarmed," Mr. Jamison said. "I saw the creature a full two minutes ago and was keeping it within sight lest it ventured too close to the horses and gave them a start. It is but a grass snake, hardly two feet long, and if I know anything of the matter, it will be more frightened of you than you are of it."

"Impossible!" Gemma said.

Gentlemanly concern warred with amusement, making the corners of his mouth twitch. "I assure you, madam, it is completely harmless."

"Of course it is, I just do not like snakes. Not since I was a child."

"Have you ever tried to conquer your fear? Perhaps if you saw the serpent up close, you might—"

"Absolutely not! Believe me, I am as close now as I wish to be. Any closer acquaintance and I might not survive the meeting."

"Gemma," Ceddy called to her. "Shall I catch it for you? It would be no trouble, I assure you. I can hold him so he cannot escape, then you could—"

"I am warning you, Cedric Creighton, do not tease me about this."

"Ceddy," his mother called, "have a care. Remember your injured arm."

The boy appeared not to hear the admonition, so occupied was he in putting first one foot then the other in front of the snake's path, his object to deter the creature's escape. When he looked up, a mischievous smile split his face. "Word of honor, Gemma, you will not die from looking at a reptile."

"So *you* say."

The boy ceased to deter the snake, choosing instead to follow it closely as it slithered nearer to the alders.

"Ceddy," Gemma called after him. "Only a disgusting chub would pursue that creature, and if you so much as *think* of bringing it back here, I warn you, I *shall* die of fright." When the lad did not stop, she raised her voice so he could not fail to hear her. "And if I expire this day, I give you fair warning, I mean to haunt you until you are a grizzled old man."

While Mr. Jamison tried to hide a smile by availing himself of his goblet of lemonade, Nora reached over and patted Gemma's hand, though her own was none too steady. "Rest easy, my love, Ceddy will not catch the creature, but even if he should, he would never frighten you with it. He has far too much regard for you to wish to see you upset."

"I hope you may be right."

Relinquishing his goblet, Mr. Jamison said, "Would you ladies feel more comfortable if I disposed of the reptile?"

Gemma gave him a telling look. "Do you refer to the snake or to my brother?"

"Gemma!" Nora said, laughing. "Shame on you." To Mr. Jamison she said, "Thank you for the offer, sir, but this is the snake's home. It is we who have come uninvited."

"I agree," Gemma said, "for I should certainly take it amiss if our situations were reversed and he—"

She stopped midsentence, for Mr. Jamison had ceased to listen. Instead, he stared in the direction Ceddy had taken. The fen carr appeared deserted, the boy nowhere in sight.

Something in the gentleman's look conveyed itself to Nora, for she called out to her son, "Ceddy, the jest has gone far enough. Come back now."

There was no answer.

"Ceddy," she called again, rising to her feet. "Where are you, Son?"

As if she had summoned him, Amos was immediately beside her, tossing aside a half-eaten gingerbread man. "I'll get him, mistress."

"Thank you, Amos. I can always depend upon you."

The words had no more than left her lips when from

somewhere in the distance a sound reached their ears; it was the pounding of hooves upon the earth. On the instant, Amos took off at a run, disappearing around the stand of alders behind which Ceddy had disappeared.

Ceddy chased the grass snake beyond the fen carr, not stopping until the reptile slithered beneath a fallen tree and disappeared entirely. When the lad turned to retrace his steps, he was surprised to discover how far he had come, almost to the narrow, wooded trail the three horses had traveled into the fen. Since he was quite familiar with his surroundings, he was not the least concerned, nor was he particularly troubled when he heard hoofbeats some little distance away. After all, what could a horse and rider have to do with him? It was while he paused to examine a deer print left recently in the spongy earth that the sounds of the galloping horse seemed to grow louder and closer.

While Ceddy waited to see who had been so unwise as to leave the trail, the horse and rider suddenly appeared, bearing down upon him at an alarming speed. The horse was lathered and a bit wild-eyed, and he was being ridden hard, his hooves digging into the soft ground and tossing the clods several feet into the air behind him.

Though the day was warm, the rider wore a dark, enveloping cape, the hood pulled down low over his forehead, and as he drew near, Ceddy saw that a cloth mask covered his entire face. Painted on the stiffened cloth was the visage of a snarling wolf, the fangs bared; the eyes had been cut out, leaving two ominous hollow slits just above the snout. More frightening than the mask was the cudgel the man held in his right hand, for while he was still several feet away, he raised his right arm, brandishing the leather-covered weapon as though he were some knight in a jousting contest.

He rode directly at Ceddy.

Too frightened to move, and believing himself doomed, Ceddy covered his head with his uninjured arm in hopes of deflecting the blows he was certain would rain down upon him at any moment. When the horse and rider were but seconds away, Ceddy heard a fearsome yell from somewhere off to his right—a yell that warned, challenged, threatened—a yell so barbarous-sounding it sent every last bird in the fen into the air. The sky was suddenly thick with literally hundreds of terrified, squawking birds, the din enough to wake the dead.

Ceddy was never to know if the horse was startled by the sound of the birds or the sight of the orange-haired giant who ran straight for him, his face filled with rage and his large hands balled into fists. As for the horseman, he gasped when he saw Amos. The gasp became a moan when the servant dealt him a crushing blow to the ribs that nearly unseated him and caused him to drop the cudgel.

The horse reared up in fear, but the rider yanked at the reins, and with the bit sawing into the sides of the poor animal's mouth, the man regained control, forcing him into submission. Unfortunately, as the horse turned, his massive head collided cruelly with Amos's back, and at the impact, the giant pitched forward, hitting the ground with a thud and landing hard on his left shoulder. When he did not move immediately, Ceddy feared he would be trampled beneath the powerful hooves.

"No!" he screamed.

Thankfully, Amos saw the danger and rolled aside with all due speed, the lethal metal horseshoes missing his head by mere inches. Immediately, the rider spurred the horse in the sides, and the animal galloped off in the direction from which they had come, the rider's cloak billowing out behind him.

As quickly as horse and rider had appeared, they were

gone, nothing left to show they had been there save the clods of dislodged earth, the servant who lay motionless upon the ground, his breathing coming in great gasps, and the cudgel the would-be attacker had dropped. When Ceddy spied the weapon, he shivered, for it lay in the grass looking more frightening, more deadly, than any snake that had ever slithered through the fen.

"Do you refer to the snake or to my brother?" Gemma had said. Duncan was still laughing at her pretended confusion over his offer to dispose of the reptile, when he became aware that Ceddy was nowhere in sight. Drat the boy! Where could he have gotten to?

While Duncan stood quite still, waiting for the lad to reappear, he heard the distant pounding of hooves upon the earth. Though a foreboding told him the boy was in danger, his logical mind argued that no one would dare harm the lad in broad daylight. Fortunately, Amos Littlejohn was unhampered by a barrister's need to weigh the facts, and the servant took off at a run. An instant later, Duncan followed suit.

Of course, Duncan's speed was nothing compared to that of the fleet-footed servant, and Amos was already well ahead of him when Duncan passed the stand of alders behind which Ceddy had disappeared.

The sounds of the galloping horse seemed to grow louder, and while Duncan pushed himself to greater speed, he heard an unearthly yell, a warning that prompted the entire bird population of the fen to take wing, their loud protestations filling the air. No less frightened than the birds, Duncan continued his headlong run. His pursuit ended abruptly when he came to a small clearing where he spotted Amos Littlejohn lying motionless upon the ground. The boy, ashen-faced and shivering, stood a few feet away, staring at something that lay upon the churned-up ground.

"Ceddy," Duncan said, not knowing to whom he should go, the boy or the servant, "are you hurt?"

"N-no, sir. Amos saved me." With tears streaming down his face, the lad turned to look toward the orange-haired giant who still lay unmoving. "Is he . . . is he dead?"

Thankfully, Amos chose that moment to moan, effectively answering the question. No less relieved than the boy, Duncan knelt beside the servant, and while he attempted to ascertain the seriousness of the injuries, Ceddy came to stand beside him, using his sleeve to swipe away the tears.

"He has damaged his shoulder," Duncan said, smiling at the lad in a way he hoped would calm his fears, "but I believe he will do. Though I doubt he will be running any races in the near future." After helping Amos to sit up, he turned to Ceddy. "Now, my boy, while your rescuer catches his breath, suppose you tell me exactly what happened."

Ceddy did as he was instructed, and by the time he finished relating his version of the incident, Amos had caught his breath and was eager to add his own account. Together they painted a clear picture of the cowardly attack, a picture that made Duncan long to put his fist through the face hidden behind the wolfish mask.

Seeing nothing positive to be gained by relating the particulars to Gemma and Nora, Duncan suggested they say only that Amos tripped and fell. "Until after I have done a bit of investigating. No point in needlessly frightening the ladies. Are we agreed?" he asked, retrieving the cudgel and placing it inside his waistcoat. "For the time being, shall we keep this incident to ourselves?"

"Yes, Cousin," Ceddy said.

Amos nodded his head several times in agreement. "Yes,

sir. Mum's the word until you find out the name of the Tom fool who was riding that horse.''

"But, Cousin, what if you do not discover his identity? Or where the horse came from?''

Duncan put his hand on the boy's shoulder. "Horses are not so easily disguised as men. I shall find both the animal and the coward behind the mask. But until I do, your mother and sister need to know only that Amos fell, hurting his shoulder, and that you are unharmed.''

Very late that same night, after the inhabitants of Howarth Manor had all retired to their respective beds, Duncan inched his way down the grand staircase, being careful not to make any noise. Though the lights had all been extinguished, leaving the corridor and steps in darkness, he was able to make his way to the front door. Once there, he slid the heavy bolt back, exited, then closed the door softly. Once he had stepped lightly across the moat bridge, he moved more quickly, heading purposefully toward the wrought-iron gates, yet staying on the lawn to avoid the crunch of the graveled carriageway.

The moon, though not yet in its full phase, cast a silvery-white brilliance over the area, supplying enough illumination to expose Duncan to anyone who might chance to be at a window. To his relief, before he had gone very far, a bank of clouds fortuitously passed before the heavenly body, dimming its beams sufficiently to allow Duncan the secrecy he wished.

He needed only a faint ray for what he planned, for he was becoming well acquainted with the mile of country lane that stretched between the iron gates of the manor and Howarth Cottage. All he asked was enough light to show him the mounting block and the service tree.

When he arrived at the cottage, all the windows were

dark save one. The dim glow of a candle showed in the front bedchamber just above the small parlor where he had found the family the day he brought Ceddy his telescope. "Drat," he muttered, staring at the curtains that fluttered through the open window, "why could she not be asleep?"

The chamber was Gemma's, he knew that, for the room to which he had carried Ceddy was to the left. Not that it mattered who was still awake, Duncan's only concern was that no one look out either of those windows.

He paused only long enough to make certain he was unobserved, then he moved quickly to his left, crossing the lane, then the open field, stopping just this side of the uncleared scrub. The place seemed deserted, but knowing that looks could be deceiving, Duncan licked his lips, pursed them, and gave a credible imitation of the clear, rich descending note of the skylark. Once the note faded into the distance, he counted to ten, then repeated the process. He was soon answered by a similar bird-call imitation.

Duncan remained silent, allowing that answering call to fade away, and within seconds a man stepped from behind the scrub, his dark clothing rendering him barely discernible from his surroundings. He was a large man, powerfully built and broad of shoulder, yet he moved with the soft-footedness of a deer, making almost no sound.

There was no exchange of greetings.

"Well?" Duncan said, being careful to keep his voice hushed. "What happened?"

"I cannot say for certain, except that I bungled the job. One minute I had him, and the next the opportunity was missed."

"Damnation!"

"I am sorry, Duncan."

"We cannot afford another such fiasco. Time is running

out. Something must be done, and done soon, before others become suspicious."

The large stranger stared at the hidden moon for several seconds, then he pushed his broad-brimmed hat to the back of his head. "What do we do now? I presume you have an alternate plan."

"I do, and this time we must not fail. This time, we must get him."

Chapter Nine

"We will get him," the large man said. "Have no fear on that score."

"Damn his eyes!" Duncan said. He reached inside his coat and removed the leather-covered cudgel. "Here. Take this."

The man took the weapon, testing its weight in his hand, giving it one soft whack across his palm. "Where did you get this?"

"Off the ground in the fen. The bastard dropped it after he tried to attack the boy. The attempt would have succeeded, too, if not for the timely intervention of Amos Littlejohn."

"Mrs. Nora Westin's servant?"

"The same. Amos is a bit slow in the *nous* box, but he makes up for those shortcomings with a sort of native canniness. The instant he heard the hoofbeats, he seemed to know that something was amiss. He wasted no time in running after the lad."

"Fleet of foot as well, is he?"

"Yes, and I thank heaven that he is. From all I could tell, he reached the boy without a moment to spare."

Duncan swore again, this time through clenched teeth. "When I think what could have happened, my blood fairly boils. The lad would not have stood a chance against a man fully grown and armed for murder. I should have been more alert."

His companion reached over and placed his big, capable hand on Duncan's shoulder. "You have every right to be angry, my friend, but not with yourself. It is I who allowed Nevil to slip away. I am solely responsible, for I underestimated the knave."

"A very crafty fellow is our Nevil."

"Very. I followed him to the village, to the Blue Lion, but there I grew careless, for when he went into the inn, I assumed he was there for a pint of ale and a bit of fun with the red-haired tavern wench. A half hour later, when I strolled into the taproom to verify that he was occupied for the afternoon, the wench was behind the bar, encouraging the advances of one of the local youths. There was not a sign of Mr. Nevil Montgomery. Blast the blackguard!"

"Do you think he knew you were watching him?"

The man shook his head. "Of that I am certain, for no one sees me unless I wish it."

It was not a boast but a simple statement of fact. Mr. Steven Yarborough had served with His Majesty's Foreign Service for several years, and one of the talents that had made him a successful operative was his ability to move about quickly and silently, being seen only when he chose to be seen. So gifted had he been at his profession that on one occasion he had actually gained admittance into Napoleon Bonaparte's quarters without being discovered.

"I was careless," Steven said. "But I will not be so again."

Nothing more was said upon that subject; instead, Duncan described the hooded cloak and the mask worn by the rider. "Nevil must have kept his room at the Blue Lion as a base for his nefarious activities. Give it a look-in; see if you can find the disguise."

"I will do so."

"I need not tell you that we need the horse as well to prove that it was Nevil at the fen."

"Then I shall find the horse as well. But not tonight, my friend. I mean to remain here until first light, to be certain no one goes near the cottage."

"Excellent. I will leave you to do what you think best; meanwhile, I will return to the manor where I can keep an eye on Nevil."

Gemma, unable to rest after the excitement of the day, had attempted to read herself to sleep. When that plan proved unsuccessful, she put her book aside, blew out her candle, and tiptoed across the colorful rag rug to the window to have a look at the stars. After pushing aside the curtains, she kneeled upon the polished oak floor and leaned her elbows on the windowsill, resting her chin in her cupped hands.

What a very strange day. Strange yet exciting. She had almost been kissed by Duncan Jamison, and as exhilarating as she found that near-event, it had been eclipsed by their ride home from the picnic. Nothing at all like their journey to the fen, the return trip had required that Gemma and Jamison share the same horse, an unconventional arrangement necessitated by a rather serious injury sustained by Amos Littlejohn.

Amos had fallen while following Ceddy, who had been so foolish as to chase after the grass snake. While pursuing the lad, Amos had tripped—just how, Gemma was never able to discover—but the fall had injured his shoulder and his knee, rendering him unable to walk back to the cottage.

Of the three horses calmly munching grass nearby, only Aries bore a gentleman's saddle, so without a moment's hesitation, Mr. Jamison surrendered the gelding. Bringing all three horses forward, he helped the servant up into the saddle and offered to lead the animal if Amos felt himself unable to ride unassisted.

"Thank you, sir, but I'll do fine as five pence. But what of you and Master Ceddy?"

"Do not worry about us," Jamison said, putting his arm around Ceddy's shoulder. "The lad and I will walk."

"No," Nora said rather quickly, looking not at Jamison but at her son. "No one need walk."

Ceddy must have felt responsible for the accident, for Gemma noticed that his face was pale and that he was unusually quiet, not having said a word since his return to the picnic site.

"Let us not stand upon ceremony," his mother continued, snatching up the blanket and stuffing it inside the picnic basket. "The logical solution is for Ceddy to hop up behind me. As for you, Jamison, I . . ." She paused only a moment, and when she spoke again, her eyes were downcast, as if she were embarrassed by what she was about to propose. "I am persuaded that Gemma will not mind sharing the filly with you. Am I right, my love?"

Not mind! It was all Gemma could do to keep her mouth from falling open in surprise. She could not believe that Nora, who was usually very respectful of the proprieties, had suggested such an unconventional arrangement. It was all well and good for Nora's son to ride double with her, his young boy's arms wrapped around her waist, but the circumstances were not at all the same for Gemma and Mr. Duncan Jamison. In the first place, they were not related. And in the second place, Jamison was not a boy but a grown man, and his were a very different set of arms!

Gemma did not answer Nora's question, she could not;

however, when she felt three pairs of eyes trained upon her, waiting for her reply, she nodded in agreement to the plan.

The ride home was even more difficult than she had feared—difficult and at the same time more exciting than anything Gemma had ever experienced.

Because of the lady's saddle, there was no question of Jamison riding forward with Gemma behind him, so he tossed her up onto the filly's back, then waited while she hooked her knee around the leather-covered saddle horn and made herself comfortable. Once she was set, he caught hold of the cantle, slipped his foot into the single stirrup, and swung his long leg over the sorrel's rump, straddling her with ease, as though he had been riding double all his life.

Gemma sat very straight, trying to ignore the fact that Jamison's right leg was flush against hers, his knee practically nestled in the bend of her knee. Even through the stiff folds of her poplin skirt, she could feel the muscles in his powerful thigh.

"Would you like to take the reins?" she asked, her voice sounding strained to her own ears.

"Not at all," he replied. "I put myself entirely in your hands."

Gemma breathed a sigh of relief. She had offered him control for the sake of politeness, but she was happy he had refused, happy to know he would not be reaching around her to guide the filly. "So," she said, as soon as she had tapped Lady's Pride to urge her to follow Nora's pretty black mare onto the narrow trail, "just how was it that Amos hurt himself?"

"Did no one tell you? He tripped." Jamison's reply was brief, almost evasive, and Gemma had the distinct impression that he was using courtroom tactics to avoid discussing the accident.

"How very odd," she said, the reference meant as much to describe Jamison's evasiveness as Amos's accident.

"Odd? Surely not, for people trip all the time."

"Not Amos. He is certainly awkward when in company, for he is ill-at-ease with strangers, but I have never known him to be anything but graceful when running or jumping. What exactly was he doing when he fell?"

"I cannot say, for I was not present. When I arrived, he was already on the ground."

"And from whence came that blood-curdling yell—the one that sent what appeared to be a million birds into the air?"

He offered no reply, and Gemma had only just drawn breath to ask another question when the filly suddenly broke into a trot, almost as if she had been kicked in the sides. Immediately, Jamison relinquished his grip on the back edge of the saddle and slipped his left arm around Gemma's waist, holding her so firmly that her shoulder blades brushed against his rock-hard chest.

She gasped, surprised by this sudden intimacy, and all else vanished from her thoughts.

"Comfy?" he whispered into her ear, his warm breath sending a shiver down her spine.

"Quite," she lied. "And . . . and you?"

"Do not be concerned for me," he said, tightening his hold on her, "for I am relaxed and totally at ease."

Gemma was certain she heard amusement in his voice, but she dared not turn around to see for herself, not with his mouth so close to her ear.

Twenty minutes had never seemed so long, and as the filly trotted along behind Nora's mare, Gemma tried to keep her thoughts centered on the black's shiny rump and swishing tail and not on the man who seemed to be wrapped around her, touching her, holding her close.

Having twice danced the waltz at the monthly Baddingham Assemblies, Gemma thought she knew what it was like to be held in a man's arms. She had been mistaken, for this closeness was nothing at all like waltzing.

Perhaps it might have been different if she and Jamison had been face-to-face. Somehow, with her back against his chest, their nearness seemed so much more intimate than she had expected—so intimate that perspiration began to trickle down her skin, with a little rivulet sliding between her breasts and stopping only when it encountered the weight of his arm as it held her around the midsection.

They were silent for some time, Jamison because he chose to say nothing, and Gemma because she could not swallow sufficiently to allow the words to leave her mouth.

"Mmm," he said finally, his cheek against the side of her head, his voice no longer hinting of amusement. "Did anyone ever tell you that your hair smells like heaven?"

Something—perhaps it was his soft breath against her cheek, or the spicy aroma of his shave cream, or the warmth that emanated from his body—induced Gemma to relax her rigid posture. As minute followed minute, a sort of lethargy took possession of her and she closed her eyes, resting her head against his shoulder. She wanted desperately to turn her head those few inches that would put her mouth next to his. Barring that, she longed to have him put both his arms around her and draw her even closer against him.

As it transpired, neither of those things happened—not the kiss or the increased closeness—for they had come to the end of the narrow, wooded trail, and as they turned onto the wider and more public lane, Jamison removed his encircling arm and straightened away from her. By then, however, it was too late, for Gemma was in a fair way of falling in love with Mr. Duncan Jamison. As for the gentleman, if he felt anything at all, he concealed the fact admirably.

When the cottage came into view, the under-groom who had waited for their return caught the filly's bridle and led her over to the mounting block. Calmly, politely, Jamison dismounted and held his arms up to Gemma to lift her down. Though the contact set her heart to fluttering within her chest, Jamison appeared unmoved. He paid her no more attention than he paid Nora a minute later when he assisted her to alight.

He remained with them only a few moments longer. When he took his leave, he was charming and courteous and said everything that was proper, thanking them for including him in the picnic and offering his hope that Amos would very soon be recovered. To Gemma's chagrin, he took no special farewell of her; he offered no private word or particular gesture to the lady who had ridden double with him.

Now, as she sat upon her bedchamber floor, gazing into the darkness that lay like a soft velvet coverlet upon the garden and the lane, she sighed. If a gentleman took no special farewell of a lady, chances were that he felt nothing special toward her. Any significance placed upon their ride, and the shared closeness, had its basis in the imaginings of a naive female—it was nothing more than a girl's flight of fancy. Duncan Jamison was handsome, wealthy, and well connected, and such a man did not fall in love with an unsophisticated country miss with nothing to recommend her but a sprinkle of freckles across her nose.

Jamison had behaved just as any other male would have done in a similar situation. He was in close proximity with a young, unattached female, and he had beguiled the time by holding her close. It had meant nothing to him. Nothing at all.

While Gemma called herself a fool for making more of the episode than she should, the clouds that had covered the moon shifted. As though someone had lit a giant candle, a silvery light swept across the earth, illuminating the garden, the service tree, and the stretch of empty field that ended with the stand of scrub.

Gemma caught her breath, for as the moonlight spread, it revealed something else as well—the silhouettes of two men who stood near the scrub. Both men were tall, but there the similarity ended, for while one of them was decidedly brawny, the other was elegantly slender. Whatever their purpose for being abroad at such an hour, the light seemed to chase them away.

The two men parted, and while the brawny one all but disappeared into the shadows of the scrub, the other one walked hurriedly toward the lane, his stride long, graceful, and athletic. As Gemma watched, she decided she had been dwelling overlong on thoughts of Duncan Jamison, for the slender silhouette appeared to fit that gentleman to perfection.

Foolish fancy, of course, for why on earth would a man like Duncan Jamison be meeting someone in a field at this time of night?

Nora Westin had been every bit as puzzled as Gemma by the accident that ended their picnic at Duddingham Fen. As well, her son had been uncharacteristically quiet following the incident, a circumstance that disturbed her more than she wished to admit. She had spent twenty minutes in Ceddy's company as they rode the mare back to the cottage, and for a loquacious boy, his answers to her questions were brief to the point of evasiveness.

As a result, Nora had lain awake for the better part of the night, wondering what had transpired when Amos had gone in search of Ceddy. Something had happened—something serious—her mother's instincts told her that much. But what could it have been?

No possible solution had presented itself during her restless hours, and when the sun began to streak the pewter sky with broad slashes of pink and purple, she decided to abandon her bed for a walk in the early-morning freshness. Dressing quickly in her old blue muslin, she twisted her long hair into a knot, securing it atop her head with a pair of tortoiseshell combs that were a gift from her first husband, then she draped a paisley shawl about her shoulders and tiptoed down the narrow stairs to the vestibule.

The front door closed softly behind her, and as Nora trod the flagstone path down to the lane, she breathed deeply of the clean, moist air, hoping it would clear her head. She had only just passed the mounting block when someone spoke to her, causing her to turn around quickly, a scream very nearly escaping her lips.

"What is amiss, lovely Lorelei?"

"Steven! Mr. Yarborough," she amended, "what are you doing here?"

"Out for a morning stroll," he replied calmly. "But what of you, ma'am? Is it your usual habit to greet the very beginning of the day?"

Nora shook her head in answer to his question, all the while regarding the broad-shouldered gentleman who had appeared from out of nowhere. *Out for a morning stroll?* Somehow she doubted the veracity of that statement. Here was no early riser. To the contrary, for from the looks of him, he had not yet sought his bed. His Devonshire-brown coat was decidedly wrinkled and his buff pantaloons bore unmistakable signs of grass stain; furthermore, if the dark stubble on his chin was any indication, he had not touched his razor for more than twenty-four hours.

"And you?" she said, looking up at him. "Are you telling me that it is your customary practice to be up at dawn?"

"Not usually, ma'am." A teasing expression flickered in his dark-brown eyes, and laugh lines crinkled at the corners. "Not unless I suspect a lovely lady might appear out of the morning mists."

"Flattery, sir? Do such tactics generally serve to distract people from asking questions you do not wish to answer?"

"I see I must be on my mettle this morning." As if invited to do so, he fell into step with her. "If you must find fault with me, ma'am, believe me to be impertinent, but do, I pray you, acquit me of any insincerity where you are concerned. To call you lovely is not flattery but self-imposed restraint, especially when there is so much more I could say."

"No, really, sir, I was not fishing for compli—"

"I might speak of your eyes," he continued, as though she had not spoken, "for they are as gray and mysterious as the waters of the Aegean." He reached out and caught a curl that had already fallen loose from the tortoiseshell combs and now hung just in front of her right ear. "Or I could mention your hair," he murmured, rubbing the strand between his thumb and forefinger, "for it is as rich and captivating as spun gold."

"Sir, I—"

"And," he added, releasing the golden tress, but not his mesmerizing hold upon her gaze, "should you forbid me from uttering such truths, my lovely Lorelei, I would obey, but not before I told you at least once how entrancing I find your beautiful face."

At his words, Nora felt a delicious warmth flow through her veins, and any doubts she may have had about his evasiveness seemed to melt in that warmth.

"I am here," he said, as if she had just asked the question, "because I spent the whole of last night in the neighborhood, completing a service asked of me by a longtime friend."

Sighing with relief, Nora said, "You did?"

"I did. I was on my way back to the Blue Lion when I

chanced to see you exit the cottage. The hour being so early, I became concerned for your welfare. Were it not so, nothing would have prompted me to appear before you in this unforgivable state of dishabille."

"Unforgivable? Not at all, sir. I . . . I am not a young girl to be offended by the sight of a man's whiskers. I am a woman grown. Twice married and twice widowed, with a young son who—"

"Whose welfare is uppermost in your thoughts."

"Yes, of course, but what mother does not keep her child uppermost in . . ." She paused, not wanting to utter an empty platitude. For some reason she did not understand and did not wish to probe, Nora wanted to tell this man of the fears that had kept her awake.

She wanted to unburden herself. Perhaps it was his size that made her wish to confide in him. She had always liked large men, and Steven Yarborough's shoulders appeared more than broad enough to support one more of the world's problems.

As if sensing her inner struggle, he spoke softly, as one might to a frightened colt, "Tell me what has cut up your peace. Perhaps I can help."

While they walked, Nora told him about her concerns for Ceddy's future and her inability to send the lad to a proper school. She even mentioned the guilt that had plagued her since she refused to allow her son to be adopted by his wealthy aunt and uncle. Throughout the entire discourse, Steven listened quietly, without making a judgment of any kind or proffering simplistic, unsolicited solutions.

Because of his attentiveness, it was easy for Nora to progress from those very specific concerns to the vague fear she had felt since the day her son had been accidentally shot. She even mentioned the uneasiness she had experienced yesterday after the picnic, though the confession obliged her to look away in embarrassment. "You will say I was foolish beyond permission, sir, for I was assured that nothing befell my son. Still, my misgivings kept me awake the entire night."

To her surprise, Steven did not treat her fears as though they were the result of a frivolous female mind. "Never disregard your instincts," he said. "It is a philosophy that has served me well on more than one occasion."

"Then you think—"

"I think," he said, "that no one can know a child so well as his mother. You have successfully guarded and guided your son for eleven years, and I have every confidence that you will continue to do what is best for him."

Inordinately reassured by this simple show of faith, Nora felt her spirits lift, and when she realized that their walk had taken them within sight of the wrought-iron gates of Howarth Manor, she suggested they turn and retrace their steps. "I, for one, have found my appetite, and if I know aught of the members of your sex, sir, you will long have been thinking of breaking your fast."

His reply was a deep, melodic laugh. "I believe, ma'am, that I could eat the proverbial sheep, wool and all."

An answering smile pulled at her lips. "What say you, then, to a stop-in at Howarth Cottage? We set a simple table—wool is seldom on the menu—but if what I hear of the food at the Blue Lion is true, then I can safely promise you a far superior meal to any you may find at the inn."

"With such a guarantee, ma'am, I should be a sapskull to refuse your kind offer."

The mile back to the cottage was accomplished in less time than the earlier, leisurely stroll, with both the lady and the gentleman agreeing that the morning was turning into a very promising day. Nora was laughing at some foolishness Mr. Steven Yarborough had offered as absolute fact when they approached the cottage door.

"A groat will net you a shilling, sir, that you have never so much as *seen* a parrot, never mind owning one and teaching it to sing sea chants."

He put his hand over his heart as if wounded. "Ma'am, you cut me to the quick."

"And," she continued, "I adjure you not to repeat that Banbury tale to my son. Otherwise, Ceddy will not be satisfied until he has such a creature in his possession so that he may teach it to—"

"Your pardon," Steven said, taking her elbow just as she was about to step across the threshold. "There is a letter of some kind on the floor, and I would not have you tread upon it and lose your footing."

Having said this, he bent down and retrieved the paper, handing it to Nora to read the name scrawled across the folded sheet.

"What on earth?" she said, accepting the missive. After discovering her own name, which was so poorly written as to be almost illegible, she turned the sheet over to break the seal, which was nothing more than a blob of common yellow wax. "Pray forgive me, sir, but I was never able to set aside a letter unread."

"By all means, ma'am. Perhaps you will discover that some hitherto unknown relative has gone to his heavenly reward, leaving you the recipient of a vast fortune."

"Would that it were so," she said, slipping her finger beneath the flap and unfolding the paper. "However, since the note bears my name but not my direction, I can only surmise that it is from some neighbor. Though how it came to be here, I cannot imagine, for . . ."

She fell silent, and after a brief interval she gasped and let the paper fall to the floor as though she could not bear to touch it a moment longer. Without asking permission to do so, Steven retrieved the sheet and read it for himself.

If you would protect your son from mortal danger, take him as far away from East Anglia as may be accomplished. Go where no one can find him. The boy's life depends upon it. Trust no one.

A friend

Chapter Ten

"How may I serve you?" Steven asked quietly.

Only after she had run up the narrow stairs to her son's room, to prove to herself that he was sleeping peacefully, would Nora allow Steven to lead her back down the stairwell and into the small informal parlor to the right of the vestibule. He bid her be seated on a worn, rose-colored settee, and when she complied, he sat beside her, holding her trembling hands in both of his. "You have but to command me, ma'am. I will do whatever will reassure you most."

When she spoke, the words were shaky and her voice sounded hollow, as if she had not yet reconciled the threat in the letter with reality. "How can this be happening? Why would anyone wish to harm Ceddy? He is just a young boy."

An idea seemed to present itself to her, for she looked up at Steven, her eyes suddenly large and round with hope. "Is it a jest, do you think? My son enjoys a running feud with the smithy's two sons. Could this be a prank got up by one of those rascals to get Ceddy into trouble?''

Steven wished he could tell her what she wanted to hear, but he respected her too much to conceal the truth. "The threat—I will not call it a warning—in that letter did not come from a child. This is the work of a grown man. A rather devious man."

Tears moistened her eyes; otherwise, she showed no surprise at his reply. "I do not know what is best to do."

"Not half an hour ago I advised you to trust your own instincts where your son is concerned. I stand by that advice. And yet," he said, squeezing her hands, "I wish to assure you that you can, indeed, trust someone. I am at your disposal, willing to act in whatever capacity you deem acceptable, ready to do all within my power to protect you and your son."

She turned her hands over so that she could lace her fingers with his. "I do trust you," she said. "But I cannot tell you what I wish, for that is something I do not know. The sad truth is that my brain seems to have shut down like one of those new steam-driven machines that has used up its allotted supply of coal."

"It is the surprise of the letter, ma'am. Take several deep breaths and expel them slowly. Grant yourself a few minutes to assimilate what has occurred, then allow time to temper the shock of the coward's words. Depend upon it, your brain will once again function."

After she had done as he suggested, breathing in and out slowly, she said, "I feel somewhat calmer, but I still do not know what is best to do."

"May I make a suggestion?"

She nodded. "I should be most grateful for the advice."

"Say nothing and do nothing for the time being, at least until you have had time to know your own wishes. With your permission, I propose to go immediately to my friend and apprise him of this threat. He and I will then devise a schedule whereby one of us will be within sight of the cottage at all times. If you should become concerned about anything, you need only open the entrance door and wave, and either my friend or I will come to you."

She sighed as though a great weight had been lifted from her shoulders. "You are very kind."

Steven gave her hands a final squeeze, then he freed them and stood, making her a formal bow. "I will go now, but if I may, I will give myself the pleasure of that promised meal another day."

"Yes, of course," she said, rising as well and following him to the vestibule. "You are most welcome at Howarth Cottage. At any time."

He lifted her hand to his lips. *"Danke schön,* fair Lorelei."

"No," she said softly, "it is I who should thank you."

Steven turned to leave, but as he did so, he recalled something she had mentioned earlier about Ceddy's morning lessons with the curate. "Does your son go to the village every day for his lessons?"

"Why, yes. He remains at home only when the weather makes travel upon the roads impossible."

"Pretend today is one of those inclement days and keep the lad at home."

Her gray eyes darkened with concern. "I do not wish my son to be frightened."

"Perhaps you could suggest that he remain at home to offer assistance to the injured servant."

"Yes. Ceddy would see nothing strange in that request."

"It is settled then. Speaking of the servant, does he have access to a pistol? Can he shoot?"

"A pistol?" Nora's face turned ashen. "We have no weapons in the house. And if Amos ever fired a pistol, I have no knowledge of the fact. Is the situation that serious, do you think?"

"No, no," he answered much too quickly. "It was but a thought, and one better left unsaid. Pray forgive me for frightening you. However," he added, stepping outside and placing his wide-brimmed hat upon his head, "now that I am leaving, I beg you will humor me by closing the door and engaging the bolt."

It was midmorning when Sir Frederick arrived at the cottage, and though he told the maid he did not wish to intrude upon the ladies while they were still at the table, the girl showed him to the small family parlor just the same. After bobbing a curtsy, she announced the visitor. "Sir Frederick Montgomery, ma'am."

Nora and Gemma both stood, not a little embarrassed to be caught breaking their fast at such an advanced hour, but neither lady could speak immediately. Nora had only just taken a bite of basted eggs, and Gemma, after pushing aside her plate of Bath buns, was obliged to lick away a comfit that had resolved to stick to her bottom lip.

Thankfully, Ceddy saved the day by tossing his napkin aside and hurrying forward to shake his uncle's hand. "Sir! You cannot know how pleased I am to see you."

If the elderly gentleman took exception to being offered a rather sticky hand, he gave no indication of it; to the contrary, the smile upon his craggy face gave evidence of the fact that he returned tenfold the lad's pleasure in their meeting. "How fortunate that I found you at home, my boy."

"My mother has declared that I am to take a day off from my studies, sir, to offer what help I may to Amos Littlejohn, our man of all work." He lowered his gaze. "Amos was injured yesterday."

"I heard something of the incident. The fellow is rallying today, I trust."

Nora, having swallowed her eggs, answered the gentleman's inquiry. "Amos is doing much better than I had expected. As a matter of fact, I was just thinking that perhaps I had been a bit hasty keeping Ceddy at home."

"That is good news, indeed," the gentleman said, "for the servant and for me, for now I am at liberty to ask if Ceddy may return to the manor house with me. I know his aunt would be pleased to have the lad drink tea with us this afternoon."

He looked rather meaningfully at Nora. "I have the chaise and four, my dear, and I shall, of course, bring Ceddy home personally."

Nora was uncertain if there was a hidden message in the gentleman's promise of personal escort, or if she had only imagined it, but she was inordinately pleased by the invitation. Firstly, because it would divert Ceddy's attention from the reasons behind this unlooked-for holiday from his studies, and secondly, because she knew he would be safe in his uncle's care.

Busy searching her brain for a way to convey to the gentleman that her son was not to be allowed outside alone, Sir Frederick solved the dilemma by stating his plans for the day.

"I had it on good authority from one of the footmen that Ceddy was adept at the game of billiards. With your permission, my dear, I should like to see for myself which of us has the steadier eye, the lad or me. After that question is settled to our mutual satisfaction," he continued, "I thought he and I might spend some time looking over the rods and reels in the equipment case."

He addressed his next remarks to Ceddy. "Mr. Titus Westin informs me that he has no interest in fishing, yet I noticed a glass-fronted case in the corner of the billiard room, a case fairly brimming with rods, reels, and all manner of tackle. Since I should like to have a go at the river while I am here, if you have no objection to helping me oil and repair enough equipment to serve our needs, I thought we might try our luck tomorrow." He paused. "Would you like that, my boy?"

"By Jupiter!" Ceddy replied, smiling broadly enough to reveal the gap in his teeth. "I should just think I would. It is course fishing, sir, and while that is not so refined as fly fishing, if we take my boat out into the middle of the river, I believe you would not find the sport contemptible."

"The very thing, my boy. I shall look forward to it."

While Ceddy hurried upstairs to change into the sack coat and nankeen breeches he wore on Sundays—attire his mother deemed appropriate for tea with his aunt—Sir Frederick assured Nora that he would not take his eyes off the boy. "Should you be worried that he might knock over a piece of Alicia's revered porcelain."

Once again, Nora had the feeling there was some hidden meaning behind the innocent-sounding promise, though she convinced herself it was but a figment of her imagination. After all, how could Sir Frederick know of the threat to her son? He could not, of course. Still, it afforded her peace of mind to know that the gentleman would keep Ceddy by his side. Her son would be safe in his uncle's care, and Nora could relax her guard for a time. She desperately needed a few hours upon her bed, hours in which to soothe away the tensions of the morning and the headache brought on by those tensions.

"Another one?" Gemma said when Nora excused herself to go up to her bedchamber to lie down. "That is two headaches within a sennight. I am persuaded you should have Mr. Finn check you over."

"If I should suffer a third attack, my love, I promise to consult the apothecary." Not waiting to see if her stepdaughter had other arguments to proffer, Nora made good her escape, quitting the parlor and hurrying up the narrow stairs.

Once inside her chamber, she drew the hangings across the window to blot out the bright sunshine, removed her dress and stays, then crawled beneath the covers, fervently hoping to lure Morpheus into bringing her sweet dreams. Unfortunately, after a full hour upon her bed, Nora was obliged to abandon all attempts at sleep. Instead, she lay quietly in the darkened room and surrendered to thoughts of Mr. Steven Yarborough, Steven and the gratitude she felt for the gentleman with the laugh lines at the corners of his eyes.

"Thank you," she whispered, her face turned heavenward, "for sending Steven just when I had need of him."

The remainder of the day was a bit dull for Gemma, who spent the time alone. Working upon her account ledger absorbed a portion of the afternoon, but when that occupation proved as daunting as usual, she abandoned it for a book of poetry. In time, the poetry went the way of the ledger, and the young lady began to feel as though her family had deserted her. That feeling was reinforced when Sir Frederick brought Ceddy home just in time for the lad to partake of his dinner.

Having had a full day, and expecting to spend all of the next upon the river with his uncle, Ceddy made short work of the meal and announced his intention of turning in early. Nora, who looked as though the afternoon spent upon her bed had yielded no benefits, was unusually quiet all through dinner, and not long after her son retired, she chose to seek the privacy of her chamber as well.

Once again, Gemma was left alone, the evening stretching out before her. Though heartily sick of her own company, she was less than pleased an hour later when she glanced out the parlor window and saw the ancient whiskey belonging to Mr. Bascombe Newley pull up beside the mounting block.

"It wanted only this," she muttered, "to turn a bad day into an abominable one."

Wishing she could think of a valid reason for refusing to receive the pompous young man, yet knowing she could not be rude to a man of the cloth, she watched while the scrawny gentleman climbed down from the gig and tied the nondescript gray mare to a limb of the service tree. Unaware that he was being observed in the gathering dusk, Mr. Newley adjusted the brim of his black hat, rubbed first one boot toe and then the other on the back of his pantaloons, then withdrew from the cane seat of the gig a bouquet of ruby-red roses fresh from the rectory garden, their stems twisted around with silver paper.

At sight of the floral tribute, Gemma groaned. She could not feign ignorance of the significance of such an offering, no more than she could pretend the bouquet was not meant for her.

"My dear Miss Westin," he began the instant the maid showed him into the room, "I had to come to reassure myself that young Cedric had not fallen ill. The occasions when the boy fails to appear for his lessons are so rare that I feared something might have laid him low."

"I thank you for your concern, Mr. Newley, but Ceddy enjoys his usual good health. Unfortunately, the same cannot be said of Amos Littlejohn, who took a rather nasty fall yesterday. Nora asked Ceddy to remain at home to be at hand should Amos need anything for which a female's presence might be inappropriate."

"Your reticence does you credit, my dear Miss Westin, for as the Scriptures inform us in the book of Timothy, verse 5, young women should be both discreet and chaste."

Gemma did not bother reiterating that it was Nora who had requested that Ceddy wait upon the servant; instead, she motioned the caller toward the settee, then she resumed her place at the round work table on the far side of the room. Taking up the embroidery hoop that lay upon the surface, she gave her attention to the plying of her needle, her main objective to avoid looking at Mr. Newley as much as possible.

The curate still clutched the roses, apparently having forgotten to present them as a token of his intentions, a circumstance Gemma hoped would outlast his visit. Her hopes were not to be realized, however, for suddenly the gentleman leapt from the settee, almost as if he had sat upon a pin. With mulish determination, he crossed the room, the bouquet preceding him by the length of his extended arm.

"These are for you," he said.

Gemma could do nothing but accept his offering, though she set the bouquet on the table immediately. "I shall put them in water directly." She did not wish to encourage him by sniffing the delicate aroma or complimenting the beauty of the dozen or so dark red buds, so she resumed her stitchery. "Thank you, Mr. Newley."

"Please, my dear Miss Westin, could you not see your way to calling me Bascombe?"

Gemma wished she were any place but in the parlor, and when the gentleman did not return to the settee but continued to stand quite near her chair, she began to search her mind for any excuse that might remove her from the small, confining room. "I hardly think it proper for me to address you by your name, sir. After all, you hold the position of spiritual leader in the neighborhood."

"But, my dear Miss Westin—dare I press my luck and call you Gemma?—you cannot be unaware that it is my most cherished wish to hold another position entirely."

He seized her hand rather clumsily and brought it to his lips, at the same time falling to one bony knee beside her chair. "The position I aspire to, my dear, dear Gemma, is that of your—"

"Sir!" she said, pulling her hand from his and rising from the table, allowing the ladder-back chair to act as a buffer between them. "Earlier you spoke of discretion. I believe you quoted from the book of Timothy."

"Yes," he said, straightening from the floor, "but what has that to do with what I wished to say to you? Surely you cannot believe my intentions anything but honorable."

He stepped around the chair and would have caught her hand again had Gemma not backed away once more, pulling another chair from beneath the table. "I would not presume to know the nature of your intentions, sir. I know only one thing, that this conversation is highly improper without the presence or approval of my stepmother."

Grasping at this rather weak gambit, she embraced it with the same fervor a drowning man embraces a lifeline. "I . . . I should not be entertaining a gentleman alone at this hour, and only your status as curate made such an interview acceptable. If, as you say, you have not come here in your capacity as spiritual leader of the neighborhood, then I must end this interview. I am persuaded you will understand, and excuse any abruptness in my manner."

Without waiting for his reply, Gemma hurried to the vestibule and opened the entrance door, holding it wide. "You will forgive me, Mr. Newley, for cutting short your visit."

Far from being wounded by her rebuff, the gentleman smiled from ear to ear, giving all the appearance of a man well pleased with his day's work. After he retrieved his hat from the console table by the door, he caught Gemma's hand and raised it to his lips for a parting salute. "My dear Gemma, your sense of propriety does you credit. I will leave now, but if you please, be so good as to inform Mrs. Westin that I shall give myself the pleasure of calling upon her at some time tomorrow afternoon."

Gemma suffered his rather clammy salute, but once he was on the flagstone footpath and she could close the door without hitting him in his skinny backside, she lifted the hem of her dress and used it to rub the back of her hand, scrubbing until the skin was quite red. "Why, why," she muttered, leaning against the smooth wood of the door, "did he have to choose this time to put his luck to the test?"

She had known for some weeks that it was only a matter of time before Bascombe Newley made her an offer, but she had hoped it would not be so soon. He had waited until her year of mourning was completed and she was once again in colors, and for that, at least, she was grateful. Now, however, the subject had been broached, and to her regret, there was no more pretending that an offer would not follow. Once he spoke to Nora, obtaining her permission to pay his addresses, Gemma would be obliged to listen to his entire proposal. Listen and give him her reply, once and for all.

Far worse than enduring the curate's proposal was forming her own reply, for her head was at war with her heart. Mr. Newley was a man of the cloth, a gentleman worthy of her respect; unfortunately, Gemma did not respect him. She did not even like him. Loving him was out of the question, and she did so want to experience that emotion—to give it and to receive it. And yet, if she refused the curate's offer, she could write *paid* beside her chances for a family and an establishment of her own, for there were no other eligible gentlemen in Duddingham.

There was also the undeniable fact that supporting three

people had put a financial burden upon Nora. Without that burden, Nora's situation would be easier; she might even be able to send Ceddy to an acceptable school, thereby assuring his future.

Gemma sighed. Could she be so selfish to Nora and Ceddy as to reject the curate's offer of his hand? Could she behave so to the two people she loved most in the world?

Not wanting to answer that question, she pushed away from the door and returned to the parlor. She did not bother to light the brace of candles that stood on the mantel, but sat down in a slipper chair beside the bare fireplace. It would be dark presently, and she could think better in the dark. If she ever needed a clear head, it was tonight.

How long she remained thus she could not say. All she knew for certain was that once she rose and went to the window, night had descended and the stars were out. The moon was at its half phase, and it cast an eerie glow upon Nora's wildflower garden.

Gemma was not certain what made her give her full attention to that unusual moonlight; perhaps it was the patterns it cast upon the small garden, or perhaps it had something to do with the color. The light was not silvery as it had been two nights ago, but rather orange-hued, and it appeared to be growing in intensity. Further, it did not come from above, but from the drawing-room window. How odd. Was the moonlight reflecting off the glass panes?

She was still pondering the oddity when she smelled smoke. The weather being warm, there were no fires lit in the cottage, but even if there had been, no prudent person would confuse the pleasant aroma of burning firewood with the foul, acrid smell that teased Gemma's nostrils. That offensive odor had but one source: burning cloth.

Her heart racing, Gemma ran to the vestibule, then let

her sense of smell lead her to the more formal drawing room. The stench had grown much stronger, and to her horror, when she stepped inside the drawing room, she saw bright orange flames licking their way up the gold-and-silver hangings at the side window.

All were dressed for the white, and broad-shouldered, and the trim and strong men, came each to the door a close. Then came a break, though it was now the last decade ... and all the while were in the file at their places across the room.

Chapter Eleven

Gemma stifled the scream that threatened to escape her throat and ran toward the window, her one thought to yank the burning hangings down before the wall caught fire and spread to Ceddy's room directly overhead. Being careful where she put her hands, she released the tieback to the left side, then pulled at the silk material. To her relief, the rod gave way easily. As ill fate would have it, the rod on the right side was not so cooperative; it refused to give way, though Gemma yanked at the hanging with all her might.

The blaze had gained such momentum that she knew she had but seconds remaining to stem this deadly menace. At any moment, the entire hanging would be engulfed in flames, and once that happened, there would be nothing left for her to do but to wake the household so they could flee for their lives.

Fear made her heart beat painfully against her ribs; even so, she tried one final time for a hold on the material, one that would not set her afire as well. She had only just touched the hot silk when a powerful hand grabbed her, the strong fingers digging into the skin of her wrist. Before she knew what was happening, she was being flung aside, . sent spinning to the floor.

"Go see to Ceddy!" a deep voice commanded.

"The flames will not have reached his room," she said. "He—"

"Go! Now!"

Far too happy to have assistance to take exception to the rough treatment or to the gruffly barked orders, Gemma picked herself up and hurried up the narrow stairs. All was peaceful in Ceddy's bedchamber. The lad looked like an angel, which proved that appearances could be deceiving, and as Gemma neared his bed, he emitted a snore worthy of a centenarian and turned over onto his side.

When Gemma returned to the drawing room, she found that her rescuer had succeeded in wrenching the rod from the wall. The hanging lay in a blazing heap of silk at Jamison's feet, and he was even then snatching up the small Axminster rug that took pride of place in front of the yellow-striped settee, using it to smother the flames.

At the time, it seemed to Gemma that the frightening incident lasted for hours. Actually, it was a case of distorted perception, for once the fire was smothered, with nothing save the odd spark needing to be stomped out, she realized that only a few minutes had passed between the moment when she first smelled smoke and the time when Jamison extinguished the final spark.

While Gemma stared at the sickening heap of black ashes, she became aware of her lungs, for they ached as if she had not drawn breath since leaving the parlor. Now, as she gulped deeply, the acrid air caused a paroxysm of coughing that racked her body.

"Here," Jamison said, taking her by the arm and leading her to one of a pair of wing chairs that flanked the garden-facing window. "Sit before you fall down." He raised the sash just enough to let in the fresh night air. "If you should begin to feel faint, lean your head out the window."

She nodded her agreement, and while she breathed in sweet, moist air, her rescuer found a candle, lit it, then set it on the small pembroke table beside her chair. Leaving her there, he went back to the side window where he ran his hands up first one wall and then the other, testing to see if the surrounding area was hot. Apparently it was not, for he came back to her and flopped unceremoniously into the companion chair. Without saying a word, he closed his eyes and rested his dark head against the padded wing of the chair, his long legs stretched out in front of him.

The gentleman's hands were covered in soot, as were his buff-colored pantaloons, and the shine on his once elegant Hessians was ruined, with the tassel from his left boot missing entirely. As well, the right sleeve seam of his bottle-green coat had burst open, and the fine lawn of his neckcloth was blackened beyond repair. Yet, he had never looked more handsome to Gemma than he did at that moment, and she was hard pressed not to fling herself into his lap and lay her head upon his shoulder.

Since no invitation was forthcoming for her to do anything even half so rash, she remained in her chair until her breathing was no longer labored. She did not move except to push aside several strands of hair that had come loose from the simple knot she wore.

In time, her thoughts became centered upon a cup of cool water and the soothing sensation the liquid would produce sliding down her throat. "Are you thirsty?" she asked. "May I offer you something cool to drink?"

At that, he opened his eyes. "Have you any brandy?"

She shook her head, dislodging the remainder of her hair, which tumbled in disarray all about her shoulders. "I am afraid not," she said, pushing the tresses behind her ears. "But I can offer you a cup of tea or a tankard of Cook's home brew."

"The ale," he said.

To Gemma's surprise, when she rose to fetch the drink, he took the candle and followed her out into the vestibule and down the short corridor to the kitchen. While she fetched the ale from the still room, he took a seat at the well-scrubbed deal table.

When she set the pewter tankard in front of him, he lifted it immediately to his lips, drinking thirstily of the creamy liquid. Only after he had drained the whole and set the empty container back down on the table did Gemma notice that the cuff of his right sleeve was charred and that the skin on the underside of his wrist was red.

"Duncan!" she said, catching hold of his filthy hand. "You have burned yourself."

The gentleman was not certain which surprised him most, the fact that he was injured or the fact that the lady had called him by his name. "So I have," he said, turning over his hand. "Do not be concerned. My man will take care of it."

"Please, I insist you allow me to put a soothing balm on it right away. It must be quite painful."

Without another word, she rose from the table and crossed the cobbled floor to a solid-looking oak dresser from which she removed a tin wash basin and a dipper. Basin in hand, she crossed to the large brick fireplace where the fire had been banked for the night. A black cast-iron pot hung from an iron crane, and using the long-handled dipper, she swung the crane outward to bring the pot within her reach. Carefully, she withdrew several dippersful of heated water.

"The water is still warm," she said, setting the basin on

the table, then fetching a cake of kitchen soap and a clean cloth. "With your permission, I will first wash away the soot so that I may ascertain the extent of your injury."

After assisting him to remove his coat, she turned the scorched cuffs of his shirtsleeves back from his wrists and forearms, folding them almost to his elbows, then she gently lifted both his hands and placed them in the warm water. Duncan suffered this treatment in stunned silence, firstly because no lady had ever ministered to him in this way, and secondly because he was experiencing unexpected pleasure from her touch.

Without warning him what she was about to do, Miss Gemma Westin dipped her own hands into the water just long enough to wet them, then she took the soap and rubbed the cake between her palms until a rich lather formed. Her next action was almost Duncan's undoing, for to his total amazement, she lifted his right hand, and using her own soapy ones, began to wash away the soot.

Slowly, gently, she rubbed her soft hands over his, smoothing her palm across his palm; then, using only her fingertips, she cleaned the back of his hand, continuing the rhythmic stroking down his fingers to the very tips. Again and again she repeated the process, stroking gently, mesmerizingly, paying special attention to each of his fingers.

Duncan closed his eyes, not moving, not daring to breathe, while her hypnotic touch cast a spell upon him, introducing into his consciousness images he had no right to be contemplating—images of her trailing those marvelous fingers over other parts of his anatomy while he buried his face in the long, sun-kissed hair that tumbled about her shoulders.

She placed his hand back in the warm water, continuing to smooth the pads of her fingers across his skin while she rinsed away the soap and soot. When she reached for the cake of soap and began to lather her hands again, Duncan decided he had better put a stop to this provocative nursing while he still had the willpower to do so.

"Never mind," he said, taking the cake from her and quickly lathering his left hand, "I can do it myself."

"Of . . . of course," Gemma said, her voice sounding odd to her own ears.

She watched him make short work of the washing, disappointed that he had needed no further assistance from her. Strangely, she had enjoyed the last few minutes, enjoyed touching him. Her skin still tingled from its contact with his, and a strange lethargy seemed to have invaded her legs, making her knees a bit wobbly. As well, her breathing was once again labored, though she did not believe the affliction had anything to do with the fire in the drawing room. As to the possibility of a fire of another kind, she decided she would do better to put such thoughts from her mind, at least until she was alone.

"If you will excuse me, Duncan, I will fetch Nora's first aid box. The balm is—"

"No!" he said rather sharply. "You have done quite enough. I believe I would do much better to let my valet see to the burn."

Gemma felt the heat of embarrassment stain her face. Had she let her feelings run away with her? Had she been too coming? Too familiar, touching him as she had done? Obviously she had given him a disgust of her; otherwise, why would he not let her continue what she had begun?

"It shall be as you wish," she said.

After he dried his hands upon the towel, he began to roll down his shirt cuffs, and to Gemma's further embarrassment, she realized that she was watching him with unseemly interest. Immediately she turned her back to him, giving him a few moments of belated privacy.

"Shall I help you with your coat?" she asked.

"Thank you, no. I believe I will do better to leave it off, especially since I am returning directly to the manor house. Before I go, however, I would like to take one last look around in the drawing room to satisfy myself that the fire is truly out."

"Please," Gemma said, suddenly cognizant of the fact that she had not even thanked him for his timely intervention, "allow me to express my gratitude to you, sir, for saving us from who-knows-what damage. I do not wish to contemplate what might have been the result if you had not happened by."

"I am happy to have been of service."

"Come to think of it," she continued. "How did you happen to be at our door at just the right moment?"

In lieu of an explanation, he reached inside his coat and withdrew a card of invitation bearing Gemma and Nora's names. "Alicia wished me to deliver this. She is making up a party to attend the Duddingham assembly tomorrow evening, and we are all to dine together beforehand at Howarth Manor."

Gemma could only stare, her brain bemused by surprise. In the year since Alicia had become lady of the manor, she had not extended to her predecessor so much as an invitation to tea, but considering everything else that had happened this evening, Gemma supposed this request for their company was not to be marveled at. "I will pass this along to Nora in the morning."

Jamison seemed not to be listening. They had reached the drawing room, and his attention was immediately claimed by the smoke-stained window and the seared carpet that still lay atop the mound of ashes that had once been the yellow-striped hangings. He crossed the room, and after a moment or two of looking around, he bent down and took a pinch of ashes between his thumb and finger and raised the particles to his nose.

"Just as I suspected," he said, sniffing the residue.

"What do you mean? What did you suspect?"

"The fire was no accident," he said. "It was set. These ashes bear the distinct odor of kerosene."

"Kerosene! If this is your idea of a jest, Duncan Jamison, allow me to inform you that I am not amused."

"Nor am I. It is my guess that someone soaked a rag in kerosene, touched a match to the rag, then placed the burning material on the window sill near the billowing hangings. By the time the silk caught fire, the villain was probably miles from the cottage, giving every appearance of an innocent man."

Gemma could not believe her ears. "Even if your conjecture is true, why would anyone wish to set a fire at Howarth Cottage? What possible gain could there be in such an act?"

He gave her a look that said, "Think about it." Then he straightened and walked back to the vestibule where he retrieved the curly-brimmed beaver that had fallen onto the floor earlier when he ran to her rescue.

"For now," he said, "you look as though you could use a good night's sleep. When I return to the manor house, I shall say only that I delivered the invitation. I will leave it to your discretion just how much or how little of what happened here tonight is made known to the general public."

With that, he opened the door and stepped outside. "Lock the door," he said, "and before you retire, close and secure the downstairs windows." It was not a request, but an order.

"I shall do as you say, though I still cannot comprehend why anyone would wish to cause a fire in our drawing room. It makes no sense. What did they hope to accomplish?"

He vouchsafed no comment, merely touched his forefinger to the brim of his hat. "Lock the door," he repeated, then turned and walked away.

Gemma shot the bolt, closed and locked the windows, then blew out the candle. She did not climb the narrow stairs to her bedchamber as Duncan had suggested; instead, she returned to the family parlor, where she went to the window to look out upon the garden and the lane beyond. She had much to sort through in her mind before she sought her bed, not the least of which were her feelings for Mr. Duncan Jamison.

"I love him," she said, making short work of that piece of deliberation. "I love him with all my soul and with all my mind, and though he cares naught for me, I know I shall never love another."

When she had begun to love him, she could not say, but she suspected the feeling might have begun the first day she saw him, when she had stood on the weir, her new dress caught on the rough wood. Duncan had freed her, not bothering to hide his mocking grin, a grin that had produced just the hint of a dimple in his left cheek. She had looked into those green eyes, with the flecks of gold near the center, and thought him the handsomest man she had ever seen. Then he had touched her, sending an awareness through her that she had not been able to forget. Nor would she forget it.

Duncan Jamison was proud and perhaps a bit quick to anger, not to mention unable to let a challenge go unanswered, but he was also funny, and kind, and gentle, and loyal, and very brave. And Gemma wanted nothing so much as to be near him.

"I love him with all my soul and with all my mind, and

though he cares naught for me, I know I shall never love another.''

This, then, was the answer to her dilemma concerning Mr. Bascombe Newley's offer of his hand. When the curate came to the sticking point, Gemma would decline his proposal. She could not consider marriage to the worthy gentleman, even if it meant she must remain a spinster for the rest of her life. Even if Duncan were to leave Duddingham on the morrow, and Gemma never saw him again, she still could not marry another. As long as Duncan Jamison lived in this world, he retained sole possession of her heart.

It was some time later when Gemma heard Nora's footfalls upon the stairs. She held a bed candle in her hand, and when she paused at the parlor door and lifted the light to see if Gemma was inside the room, her flowing white wrapper gave her almost a spectral appearance.

''My love,'' she said, ''why are you sitting in the dark?'' Not waiting for the answer, she began to sniff as if only just noticing the acrid odor that permeated the downstairs area. ''What is that vile smell?''

''The drawing room,'' Gemma replied.

In the few moments before Nora spun around and hurried across the vestibule, her countenance seemed to turn a sickly white, almost as if she had a premonition about what she would find in the other room. Concerned, Gemma sped after her.

A strangled gasp was Nora's first reaction, then she began to tremble. ''Heaven preserve us,'' she whispered, ''he will stop at nothing.''

Not wanting to fight a second fire, Gemma took the candle from Nora's trembling fingers, then she put her arm around her stepmother's shoulders. "He?" she asked. "Who do you mean?"

"The villain who committed this vile act. The . . . the man who wishes to kill my son."

Having uttered the words, Nora went limp and crumpled to the floor in a faint.

Chapter Twelve

"Why did you not tell me?" Gemma asked, pacing the short length of the family parlor, then turning to retrace her steps. Fear for Ceddy, coupled with her frustration at being kept in the dark about the threats upon the boy's life, made her voice sound more strident than she meant it to be. "How could you not apprise me of the possible danger?"

Nora, though empathizing with her stepdaughter's fear, sought a momentary respite behind the cloth Gemma had soaked in water scented with lemon verbena. She pressed the cool cloth against her warm face and rested her head against the cushion Gemma had placed behind her head. "Forgive me, my love, but I needed time—time to sort out my own feelings. I only just discovered the whole this morning, when the letter arrived."

"Letter? What letter?" Gemma muttered something quite unladylike. "A stranger might be forgiven for thinking me away from home for the past sennight, so uninformed as I am upon matters pertaining to my own family."

Nora took the rebuke in good part, not attempting to justify her actions. "Look there," she said, pointing to the small console table that stood beneath the window. "The letter is in the drawer."

Gemma wasted no time in retrieving and reading the short missive. "Mortal danger?" she said aloud, going over the few lines a second time. "His life depends up it? Trust no one?" She looked up from the single sheet, relief writ plainly upon her countenance. "Nora, my dear, surely you did not take this seriously. A groat will net you a shilling this was sent by one of those rascally boys in the village. Depend upon it, this is a boy's prank. One has only to look at the atrocious handwriting. I need not even mention the wording, for it is too melodramatic by half."

"The words may be melodramatic, but Steven judged the writer to be quite serious. More than serious, actually, for Steven believes the letter was meant not as a warning but as a threat upon Ceddy's life."

"Steven? Who is Steven? And what has some person I never heard of got to do with this letter, or, for that matter, with us?"

A blush stained Nora's cheeks. "Mr. Steven Yarborough," she said. "I . . . I made the gentleman's acquaintance the morning of the picnic, when I remained home from church."

Gemma could only stare. "But that was the day you had the headache. I understood you meant to return to your bed."

Nora blushed again. "I had meant to, but I went into the garden instead. It was there I met Mr. Yarborough."

Not certain she liked the idea of Nora becoming acquainted with a gentleman whose name brought color to her cheeks, Gemma persisted. "And today's headache, had it anything to do with this Mr. Yarborough?"

"If you please," Nora said, her blushes gone and her

chin raised slightly, showing signs of obstinacy, "let us leave the subject of Mr. Yarborough for another time. At the moment, it is this threat to Ceddy we must address, for I assure you, *I* consider the matter of prime importance."

"Of course it is. Pray forgive me, Nora, if I led you to believe that Ceddy's welfare is not always uppermost in my mind." Not having missed the coolness in her stepmother's usually warm voice or the resolute lift of her chin, Gemma added, "Your pardon as well, if I overstepped my bounds. I had no right to criticize your actions."

"No, no," Nora said, waving away the apology. "It is I who should ask your pardon, for I suspect that what I am about to say will distress you. Even so, I beg you will hear me out."

"You may say anything to me, Nora, no justification needed."

"Very well, my love. Bear with me, if you will, while I share with you the thoughts that have assailed my brain since early this morning. No, I must correct myself, for I spoke in the plural when it is one 'singular' thought that has repeatedly presented itself in a logical light."

"I congratulate you upon discovering even one logical thought, for the more I hear of this affair, the more illogical it all sounds to me. I cannot imagine why anyone would wish to harm a young boy. Especially not a likable youngster like Ceddy!" She glanced down at the sheet of paper she still held. "If, as you believe, this is no jest, what can Ceddy have done to incite this villain to such threats?"

"My son has done nothing. But consider, if you will, what others have wished to do for him."

Gemma shook her head. "I do not follow your reasoning. Who—"

"Sir Frederick and Lady Montgomery," Nora replied. "Surely you recall that Ceddy was shot the very next day after his aunt and uncle came to ask me if they might adopt the boy and make him their heir.''

Gemma's mouth fell open. ''Oh, my. It was, indeed, the very next day. Because you refused Sir Frederick's offer, I had not made the connection between the accident and the Montgomery fortune. In fact, I asked Jamison earlier this evening what anyone might hope to gain by setting the cottage afire. At that time, however, I thought of us—you, me, and Ceddy—as being poor as church mice, totally dependent upon your three hundred pounds per annum.''

''Which, indeed, we are, for no matter the financial inducement, I could not allow Sir Frederick to adopt my son and take him away.''

''Naturally you could not. Anyone acquainted with you would know you could not give up your child.''

''But,'' Nora continued, ''suppose the person who wrote that letter has no knowledge of me or of my sincere attachment to Ceddy? What if the person—whoever he may be—is under the impression that I welcomed the offer, and that Ceddy will very soon figure as Sir Frederick's heir?''

As if her legs would no longer sustain her, Gemma sat down upon the edge of the settee, letting the letter drop from her limp fingers. When she spoke again, her voice was hesitant, as though she would rather ask anything than her next question. ''Why . . . why would this person—whoever he may be—care who was chosen heir, unless . . . unless he believed he had a prior claim to be so designated? A claim he wished to protect no matter what was . . .''

''No matter what was required of him,'' Nora finished for her.

''No!'' Gemma replied, shaking her head, the action reminding her that her hair still hung about her shoulders. Impatiently she pushed aside the strands that fell across her face. ''I cannot—nay, I will not—credit this to be true, for other than Ceddy, Sir Frederick has but two living relatives."

"His nephews," Nora said, stating what they both already knew. "Mr. Nevil Montgomery and Mr. Duncan Jamison."

Gemma felt as though some giant fist had dealt her a severe blow to the chest, causing her heart to ache unbearably, and she was obliged to take a steadying breath before she could speak. "You cannot believe that Duncan would do anything to harm Ceddy."

Nora could not meet her gaze. "I do not *wish* to believe it of him, for I have become used to thinking of him as a friend, but allow me to relate to you the three things that I have been reviewing again and again in my mind this entire day."

Without waiting for Gemma's reply, Nora touched her right forefinger against the tip of her left forefinger. "Firstly, there is the matter of the accident in which Ceddy was shot. If you will recall, Mr. Nevil Montgomery had not yet arrived in Duddingham at that time. On the other hand, Jamison accompanied Sir Frederick and Lady Montgomery upon their journey. As well, he knew of his uncle's intention to name Ceddy as his heir. We cannot be certain that Nevil knows anything of the business even now."

Feeling on safer ground here, Gemma hurried to remind Nora that Jamison was with *her* when Ceddy was shot. "I told you how I chanced to meet him at the bridge when I was returning from the village. Surely you remember me relating to you the circumstance of our meeting Mr. Newley upon the road. Mr. Newley brought me home in his gig, but it was Duncan who walked with me to the door. He and I were together when he chanced to discover Ceddy beneath the rose arbor."

"My son was unconscious when you found him, and he had lost a great deal of blood. Who can say how much time had passed between the actual shooting and your discovery of him? Was it sufficient time, do you suppose, for a man on horseback to gallop three miles to the village, then return?"

When Gemma made no reply, Nora touched her second finger. "There is also the matter of the fire in the drawing room."

"But Duncan came to my rescue."

"Very true, but I believe you said he appeared *after* you discovered the fire and had begun to put it out. An interesting coincidence, was it not, that he just happened to be at hand to lend his assistance?"

"It was certainly a fortuitous one!" Gemma added.

"That I shall not dispute, my love, for I should have been devastated if you had sustained an injury while putting out the flames. However, one must be forgiven for wondering why Jamison was in the area at such an hour?"

Gemma could sit still no longer and rose abruptly from the settee. "You are misreading this, Nora. Duncan explained to me his reason for being just outside the cottage. He had come to bring us an invitation from Alicia."

"An invitation?" Nora's eyebrows lifted in patent disbelief. "I cannot credit that any invitation, even one from Alicia Westin, is so important it must be delivered by moonlight, and by a guest of the house. Are there no servants at the manor to send upon such errands?"

Nora's question hung in the air between them. Her observations had been reasonable, disturbingly so, and after what seemed an eternity of unrelieved silence, Gemma spoke, her voice subdued. "You mentioned three things that had occupied your thoughts today, yet you have ticked off only two. What was the third?"

" 'Tis the picnic, or rather, the accident at the picnic."

Feeling on safer ground here, Gemma spoke with more assertiveness. "But it was Amos who was injured, not Ceddy. Amos fell," she added.

"In any event," Nora said, "that is the story you and I were told. Though even at the time, I felt that something was being withheld from us, especially when none of the three males seemed eager to give us a full account of the incident. Furthermore, did you not notice Ceddy's behavior afterward—how uncharacteristically quiet he was?"

Gemma had not noticed Ceddy's behavior, for her full attention had been upon Mr. Duncan Jamison and the strong, masculine arm that was wrapped tightly around her waist. Now, however, she recalled having the feeling all during that very intimate horseback ride that Duncan was trying to keep her from asking him questions.

"After thinking over that afternoon," Nora continued, "I am convinced that whatever befell Amos happened to him only because he arrived in time to defend my son from an attack of some kind."

"And Duncan?"

Nora sighed. "Yet again, Mr. Jamison was close at hand."

"But Amos arrived upon the scene first," Gemma insisted. "And until the moment when Duncan gave chase, he had not been out of my sight for the past hour. Reason must tell you that he could not be in two places at once."

"You are right, of course, but what if he had the aid of an accomplice?"

Accomplice. The word had a sinister sound, and as Gemma repeated it to herself, she was immediately reminded of the two men she had seen silhouetted in the moonlight last evening. Foreboding gripped her like a vise, making it difficult for her to breathe.

"You have thought of something," Nora said, rising from the chair and crossing the room, stopping before Gemma.

"No, I—"

"Do not bother to deny it, for your eyes give you away." She grasped Gemma firmly by the shoulders. "You must tell me what you know. Otherwise, how am I to protect my son?"

Though the telling of it made Gemma physically ill, she related the moonlit incident to Nora, leaving nothing out. "They stood together for several minutes," she said, "apparently deep in conversation. Then, as if by mutual consent, the larger man disappeared behind the scrub, while the slender gentleman turned and walked toward the lane. As I watched him walk away, something in his bearing made me think for a moment that it might be Duncan."

Nora's hand went to her throat, as though she, too, felt unwell. "And the other man?" she said. "Did you recognize him?"

"I did not, for I have never seen him before."

"You are certain?"

Gemma nodded. "Depend upon it, I would not have forgotten such a person, for he was one of those big, very capable-looking men."

"Big?" Nora repeated, the single word seeming to stick in her throat.

"Yes. Tall and quite broad in the shoulders, and very . . . Oh, what is the word I am searching for?"

"Brawny?" Nora suggested, her voice just above a whisper.

"Exactly," Gemma said. "The very word."

While two very melancholy ladies adjourned to their respective bedchambers, each with a heavy heart, the two gentlemen responsible for the despondency met across the lane near the scrub. The brawny gentleman approached the area, giving a credible imitation of the clear, rich descending note of the skylark; then, once the note faded into the darkness of the night, he counted to ten and repeated the process. Immediately there came an answering bird call.

"Your timing is excellent," Duncan said, his voice hushed, "for I have need of you."

"What has happened?"

"First, tell me, were you successful in locating the horse ridden by the person who tried to attack Ceddy in the fen?"

"Not yet, but I bribed the landlord at the Red Lion, and he gave me the name of a farm nearby where, for a price, a man might hire a horse with no questions asked. I mean to pay the farmer a visit on the morrow."

"And the disguise the man wore, the mask and cloak?"

Steven shook his head. "I managed to have a look inside the room your cousin hired for the week, but I found nothing there save a pile of soiled linen awaiting the services of the inn laundress."

He paused, then sniffed the air. "Speaking of linens, you will forgive me, old boy, but yours smell a bit charred. Have they suffered a mishap?"

"You could say that. Not more than an hour ago, I was obliged to assist Miss Westin to put out a fire at the cottage. One, I might add, that began in the drawing-room window, the catalyst for the blaze a rag soaked in kerosene."

"Devil a bit!"

"My sentiments exactly."

"The boy?"

"Unharmed," Duncan said. "He slept through the entire episode."

Steven exhaled loudly. "Thank heaven for that. But I have to wonder how many more of these near misses the lad can survive. Or, for that matter, how many more his mother can withstand with any degree of calm."

"I have been pondering both those questions this hour and more, and I have decided that we must get Ceddy away to some safe place, a place where he can be guarded from within. These outdoor vigils are not effective enough; not if someone can set a fire beneath my very nose without being detected."

"You are right, of course. Have you a place in mind to take the boy?"

Duncan nodded. "I thought of Montgomery Park. If my uncle were to invite Ceddy and the ladies for a visit to Chelmsford, it would occasion no remark if I came along for a visit as well."

"And I would be but minutes away at the grange."

"My thoughts exactly. I am certain Sir Frederick will agree to the scheme. My only regret is that we cannot set out for the park first thing tomorrow."

"Why can you not?"

"It is Alicia, our hostess. She has got up some curst dinner party for tomorrow evening, to be followed by a look-in at the local assembly. I am certain my aunt will say we cannot possibly be so rude as to accept the lady's hospitality then take our leave before her one planned entertainment."

"Deuce take the woman and her entertainment! Speak with your uncle. Have him explain the situation to Lady Montgomery. Depend upon it, her ladyship will know how to refuse the entertainment without giving offense. A very knowing lady is your aunt, and my guess is, she will also have an idea how the ladies at the cottage are to be got around. Though, in all candor, I am persuaded they should have been told what you suspected from the outset."

"It was my hope to protect them for anxiety until such time as I had proof of Nevil's involvement in Ceddy's misadventures."

Steven put his hand on Duncan's shoulder. "My friend, females are not nearly so fragile as we males choose to believe. And though your intentions were kindly meant, I suspect that when Mrs. and Miss Westin discover to what extent you have 'protected' them, they will not thank you for it.''

They will not thank you for it.

Steven's words repeated themselves inside Duncan's head during the walk back to the manor house, and not even the sudden clap of thunder that reverberated through the sky could rid him of the suspicion that his friend might be in the right of it. Gemma and Nora Westin were both intelligent women, and now that he thought about it, he saw a distinct possibility that they might consider his actions as meddling in their affairs.

Another clap of thunder sounded, and, with it, a bolt of lightning lit up the sky, the lane, and the wrought-iron gates up ahead. Though large, cold raindrops began to spatter Duncan's hat and shoulders, he gave little thought to the elements; he was much too caught up in his recollection of the events of the evening—the fire, and the terror that had all but overwhelmed him when he ran into the cottage and spied Gemma battling the flames!

For just an instant he had stood transfixed, as if pinned to the spot by the horror of what he saw, unable to move. While he watched her yank at the blazing window hangings, a sickening fear began in the pit of his stomach and spread throughout his body—a fear that at any moment the burning silk would give way and fall down upon her head, engulfing her in flames.

It had seemed an eternity before he reached her to fling her aside, out of harm's way. Even now, when he thought of what might have happened to her, his hands shook, and he was forced to ball them into fists to still the tremors. At the action, the skin of his right wrist rebelled, and he was reminded of Gemma's attempt to tend his wounds.

"Heaven help me," he muttered, "for her way of washing hands nearly started a second fire!"

After the danger from the flaming drapery had been dealt with, and he and Gemma sat in the companion chairs by the front window, each struggling to force fresh air into their lungs, Duncan had ached to take her into his arms, to hold her close and reassure himself that she was unharmed. Gemma with her sky-blue eyes and her sunny blond hair, and the sprinkle of angel kisses that were smudged with soot from the fire. He had been about to cast caution to the wind when she offered him a cool drink. He had readily accepted the offer, happy to have been saved from possible entanglement.

Then she had washed his hands, and it had been all Duncan could do to remove himself from temptation, for Gemma Westin was not the kind of woman a man kissed and then forgot. Furthermore, from the way his body had reacted to her touch, he doubted that one kiss, or even a thousand kisses, would have been enough to cool his ardor.

As for forgetting her, that would not be so easy to accomplish, either, with or without the kisses. In the time Duncan had been in Duddingham, he had come to know Gemma Westin—know her and admire her—and though she was totally unsuited to be a politician's wife, the idea kept sneaking into his brain that a lifetime spent with Gemma might be filled with the kind of love he had never expected to find.

By the time Duncan reached the iron bridge that spanned the moat, the rain was coming down in earnest, pelting him with icy nuggets and soaking him to the skin, and he wondered, fleetingly, if Amos Littlejohn had predicted this downpour. Of far more importance than the arrival of the deluge, however, was its possible duration. If the rain continued for days, as it had done in the previous week, the roads between Duddingham and Chelmsford would be unusable, and the journey to Montgomery Park would, of necessity, be delayed.

A flash of lightning revealed the entrance door to the manor house, but Duncan was not obliged to sound the big brass gargoyle knocker. While he was still on the bridge, the butler threw open the door.

"Sir," he said, "you are soaked through. Shall I send word to the kitchen to bring up hot water for a bath?"

"Perhaps later. For now, where may I find Sir Frederick?"

Chapter Thirteen

"What is it, Amos?" Gemma asked, stopping just inside the cobble-floored kitchen. "What have you there?"

Gemma had abandoned the tedious, sneeze-producing task of sprinkling powdered talc inside the leaves of the more valuable books upon the parlor shelves and come to ask Cook for an early nuncheon. The use of the powdered talc was necessitated by the four days of unceasing rain that had left everything in the cottage smelling musty with damp, but the request for an early meal was for Nora's sake; Gemma hoped it would give her stepmother something else to think about. Nora was in a bad way, jumping at every sound, and her nerves were stretched almost beyond their endurance by her growing fear for her son's safety.

Unfortunately, Cook was nowhere in sight; the kitchen was empty save for Amos, who held a piece of folded paper in his hand. The orange-haired giant, unable to read, shook his head in answer to her question. "Don't rightly know what it is, Miss Gemma. Somebody slipped this paper under the kitchen door. Thought it might be a billy-doo for Betsy from one of the lads at the manor stable—she gets 'em from time to time—but now I b'aint so sure.''

Only mildly interested, Gemma took the folded sheet, which had gotten damp around the edges, and read the name printed in block letters upon the front. "Your senses have not failed you," she said. "This is not for Betsy. It bears Ceddy's name."

"Master Ceddy be in his room. You want I should take it up to him, miss?"

"Thank you, no. I will give it to him later." Having said this, she slipped the missive inside her apron pocket, putting it out of sight and out of mind. "For now, I am come to speak to Cook. Do you know where she is?"

"Her and Betsy be in the attic, miss, searching out leaks in the roof. Found some, too, that be why she sent me down, to fetch another bucket and some rags."

"Oh, dear, let us hope one bucket will suffice. Naturally, I would not think of disturbing Cook when she is involved in so important a chore, so I shall take myself back to the parlor and to my own task and try for a little patience."

Amos touched his finger to his forelock. "Yes, miss."

"By the way," Gemma added, before he left her to seek the required bucket and rags, "have you any notion when this rain will end? I should like to know if we need to start building an ark and gathering in the animals two by two."

Even Amos understood that biblical reference, and he laughed aloud. "No need for that, miss. The rain'll be ending real soon now. Though I'd stay away from the river for a few days, on account of it's bound to be swollen. But if you do go there, remember the weir b'aint new as it used to be. Mayhap it'll be weakened by all this rain, so mind you don't stand on it, else you could be the wetter for it."

"I shall heed your warning, Amos, though I doubt I shall go anywhere near the river. In fact, when I do venture outside, I probably will not walk any farther than the end of the flagstone footpath, not until the ground has soaked up all this rainwater.''

Happy to hear that the downpour would soon end, Gemma returned to the parlor, but when she arrived, Nora was no longer there. It did not require a genius to guess where her stepmother had gone, for every few minutes the lady found some task that would take her abovestairs so that she might reassure herself that her son was still in his room, unharmed.

True to Amos's prediction, the rain ceased to fall within the hour, and very soon, what sounded like an entire colony of lapwings landed atop the rose arbor. The birds could be heard calling to their feathered friends, possibly discussing the unsuspecting earthworms they would enjoy once the puddles in Nora's wildflower garden were so obliging as to drain away.

As for the owner of the garden, her appetite was not nearly so voracious. In fact, she scarcely touched her nuncheon, though Cook had prepared a fricassee of chicken accompanied by escalloped apricots, one of Nora's favorite meals. The lady was too nervous to eat, and because she was on the alert for every sound, it was she who first heard the approach of their visitor late that afternoon.

"Who is that?" she asked, almost dropping her embroidery frame. Before Gemma could reply, Ceddy jumped up from the floor where he worked a puzzle and ran to the window.

"It is Cousin Duncan. Famous!" he said, hurrying toward the vestibule.

"Ceddy," his mother ordered, halting his steps, "please close the door and take your seat."

"But, Mother, it is—"

"You heard me, Ceddy."

The lad obeyed, closing the parlor door, but while he

looked from his mother to Gemma, confusion replaced the earlier smile upon his face. Gemma was in total sympathy with his feelings, for she was still in a state of shock herself, unable to reconcile what Nora had told her of Duncan Jamison's villainous plans with what she felt for him in her heart. She said nothing of this, however, merely placed her finger across her lips, warning Ceddy to silence.

"Sorry, sir," Amos said, denying them to the visitor, "but the ladies b'aint receiving today."

Gemma heard Duncan laugh good-naturedly. "Are you quite certain? Perhaps if you told Mrs. Westin that I bring a message to her from Lady Montgomery, she might reconsider."

"Your pardon, sir, but I've got my orders. The ladies b'aint receiving."

"And what of Ceddy? Is the lad not receiving as well?"

"No, sir. I mean, yes, sir. That is, Master Ceddy b'aint receiving neither."

Ceddy's mouth fell open. "Mother? What—"

"Shh."

"But—"

"Be silent," she whispered. "I will not tell you again."

The boy could not have been more surprised if his mother had suddenly grown a second head, but he obeyed her command and remained silent.

"If you will," Jamison said, his voice noticeably cool, "please give this letter to Mrs. Westin, with my compliments. And be so good as to tell *Miss* Westin that I shall return tomorrow, at which time I hope she will be at home to visitors."

"Yes, sir."

They heard the entrance door close, followed by the sound of footfalls outside upon the flagstones, then a moment later Amos scratched at the parlor door.

Ceddy looked at his mother, who nodded her head, giving him leave to let Amos come in.

"You have a letter for me, Amos?"

"Yes, ma'am."

Amos's face had grown quite red, and from the way he kept his eyes downcast, it was obvious the giant had not enjoyed the task of turning away a man he considered a friend of the house. Still, his loyalty was to Nora, so he did not question her orders; instead, he crossed the room, handed over the two folded sheets of vellum, then he turned quickly and exited the parlor.

"Mother," Ceddy said, his voice hushed, "why did you have Cousin Duncan turned from the door? Was it the mess he left in the drawing room? Are you angry with him for ruining your good carpet?"

Nora shook her head. "The carpet was only a thing. When faced with real danger, one does not lament the loss of such items."

"Then I do not understand. Since it was my cousin who put out the flames, does that not make him a hero? Should we not be grateful to him? After all, if he had not been here, the entire cottage might have burned to the ground."

At his words, a shudder ran through Nora. Gemma, aware of how stressful the last five days had been to her stepmother, went to Ceddy and put her arm around the boy's shoulders. "Will you trust your mother and me and not ask any more questions? She and I need to talk, and after we finish, one of us will come up to your room and explain everything to you."

"But—"

"Please," Gemma said, "just give us this time."

Ceddy looked as if he would like to argue, but after glancing at his mother's pale face, he nodded his agreement and left the room. He ran up the stairs at a pace that would normally have earned him a reprimand,

and when he slammed his bedchamber door, Gemma did not flinch. Actually, she would have slammed a few herself, if she'd had the least faith that it would relieve her heavy heart. Quite certain that nothing would help her, she returned to Nora's side.

"Read your letter," she said.

Nora lifted the sheets that bore Lady Montgomery's neat copperplate. After breaking the wafer, she unfolded the crisp vellum and began to read silently. "Her ladyship wants us to accompany them when they return to Chelmsford."

"Us? You and Ceddy, do you mean?"

"All three of us. She proposes a stay of unspecified length. 'For as long as it shall please you,' she says."

Nora finished the first page and turned to the second, but as she perused that sheet, her hands began to shake. "'Sir Frederick will hire a post chaise,'" she read aloud. "'You, Miss Westin, Ceddy, and I will travel in the chaise and four, leaving the hired equipage to my husband and our nephew, Duncan, who plans to join us at Montgomery Park for a week or so.'"

At the words, something like an icicle pierced Gemma's heart, leaving her feeling bruised and cold to the very core of her soul. It was torment to her to believe that the man she loved could harm a child, especially when everything within her rebelled at believing he would harm anyone. If it had been only her own safety in question, she would have taken that leap of faith and trusted in Duncan. The risk was not to her, however; it was Ceddy whose life was in danger, and for that reason, Gemma dared not go against the evidence of her head.

"What are we to do?" Nora asked, tears coursing down her cheeks. "How are we ever to keep Ceddy safe? We are two women, alone and with almost no resources, and Jamison is a man of power and connections. Who would believe our story? How is such a man—such a threat—to be eluded? I know it cannot be done."

It cannot be done. Somehow, hearing those words of defeat from Nora, and watching her tears, sent a surge of anger through Gemma, anger so hot it melted the icy coldness that had settled in her chest. *How dare anyone threaten Ceddy and Nora? How dare they inflict pain upon the kindest, dearest woman Gemma had ever known?*

"You are right," Gemma replied, "the threat cannot be eluded. Therefore, we must face it head on. Now dry your tears, there's a good girl, and listen to my plan, for I believe there is a way out of this dilemma."

Nora brushed aside the tears, apparently encouraged by the sound of resolve in her stepdaughter's voice. "What is your plan?"

"It is very simple, actually, for we have overlooked the most elementary and logical solution."

"Please, tell me."

"We call everyone together—Sir Frederick, Lady Montgomery, and both their nephews—and you tell them in no uncertain terms that you do not wish your son to be named as heir to Montgomery Park. Never. Tell them that if they should persist in this plan, you will take Ceddy away where they will never see him again. When his aunt and uncle realize that you are serious, I am certain they will withdraw their offer. Once Ceddy no longer figures as an impediment to Dunc—to either of Sir Frederick's nephews receiving a handsome inheritance, I believe all will be well."

"Gemma," Nora said, hurrying to embrace her, "why did we not think of this before! It is the very thing, my love. I shall write to Lady Montgomery this very minute, explaining that we must all meet. What say you to tomorrow?"

"The sooner the better," Gemma said, returning Nora's

hug, then disentangling herself. "Tomorrow is the Sabbath, but I doubt the lane will be dry enough to allow anyone to drive to the village for services."

"Then tomorrow it shall be. Once I have finished the letter, I will send Amos to the manor house to deliver it."

"After that, Nora, I beg you will explain the whole to Ceddy. He may be a child, but he knows something is amiss, and being left in ignorance will only lead him to come to his own conclusions—conclusions that may prove more painful than the truth."

"You are right, of course. The instant the letter is written, I will go to my son and tell him as much as I think he can understand."

Having determined upon a course of action, both the Westin ladies felt immeasurably better, and when Nora quit the parlor to go to her own chamber to compose her letter, Gemma set about returning the books to the shelves and putting away the powdered talc and the pounce bag she had used to dust the powder between the pages.

It was while she was removing her apron that she heard a crackle in her pocket and remembered the note Amos had found slipped beneath the kitchen door. As she reread the block letters that spelled out Ceddy's name, Gemma recalled the threatening letter Nora had received five days ago. This handwriting was nothing like the scrawl used before, but Gemma suddenly felt compelled to read this missive before handing it over to Ceddy.

Breaking open the blob of sealing wax, she read:

My dear Cedric,
You do not know me, but I was a friend of Charles Creighton,
your father. Before Charles died, he gave me something to
give to you, and I have waited far too long to discharge
that commission. Not far from your home there is a weir

*that crosses the River Nene. Meet me at that weir at six of
the clock. It must be today, for I leave East Anglia tomorrow.*

Yours etc.

There was no signature, only the salutation, and without
questioning her conclusion, Gemma knew there was also
no unfulfilled commission from Charles Creighton. It was
all a diabolical scheme to lure Ceddy to the river. She
would not allow herself to linger overlong on the identity
of the man who had devised that scheme; even so, tears
filled her eyes and a tightness invaded her throat, making
it difficult for her to swallow.

"Why?" she whispered, as though Duncan were there
to hear her question. "Why did you have to prove to be
a villain? I could have loved you for all the years of my
life, and drawn what comfort I might from that love, one-
sided though it may have been. But now, you have taken
even that consolation from me. Now I must expunge you
from my heart as well as from my life.

"And the sooner the better!" she said, repeating the
advice she had given Nora.

Angrily, she swiped at the tears that would not be held
at bay, tears that insisted on brimming over and spilling
down her cheeks.

Turning to look at the bracket clock that sat on the
mantel, Gemma saw that it wanted but ten minutes to six.
With no other thought than to tell Mr. Duncan Jamison
exactly what she thought of a villain such as he, so she
might erase him from her consciousness forever, Gemma
hurried to the kitchen where rubberized coats and hats
hung from pegs near the rear door. After strapping on a
pair of pattens to raise her half-boots an extra two inches
above the level of the mud, she donned the smallest of
the raincoats, pulled one of the hats down low on her
head, and exited the cottage.

After making her way around to the front of the house and past the rose arbor, Gemma headed toward the lane, her wooden pattens making a clicking noise upon the still-damp flagstones. Crossing the lane was not easy, for the mud was deep and viscous, often coming up over the toes of Gemma's boots, but walking across the expanse of land beyond the scrub was almost impossible.

Springy at the best of times, the sloping ground that led to the river now resembled nothing so much as a bog, and it seemed determined to suck Gemma's feet into its depths—boots, pattens, and all. Traversing the final quarter mile was a veritable tug-of-war, for after each step, she was obliged to use both hands to extricate her back foot from the suction of the mire.

Pausing beside one of the scraggly little goat willows to catch her breath, Gemma glanced down toward the river. As Amos had foretold, the Nene was swollen well beyond its banks, and the usually placid blue waters moved rapidly, muddied and roiling beyond recognition.

Of the man she had come to meet, there was no sign, though she supposed he might be waiting on the other side of the tall, thick hawthorn bush. It was difficult to see clearly, for the sky was gray and the day darker than usual for the hour.

When she finally drew near the hawthorn, she saw the silhouette of a tall, slender gentleman who waited on the other side. He wore a heavy, dark cloak that reached to his boot tops, the hood pulled down low over his forehead, and his back was to her, as though he studied the weir. As for the wooden structure, Gemma was reminded of Amos's warning that the weir was old and might be weakened by the rain. "Mind you don't stand on it," he had said, "else you could be the wetter for it."

Amos need not fear, for Gemma had no intention of going near the thing. It had been dilapidated prior to the heavy rains, but now water surged through the wooden slats with a force she had never witnessed before. As well, the level of the dammed-up waters was almost even with the top of the barrier, and if the torrent did not abate soon, there would be nothing left showing of the weir save the splintery hand rails.

The noise of the turbulent river covered Gemma's approach, and as she rounded the hawthorn bush, she was obliged to raise her voice to gain Duncan's attention.

"Jamison!" she yelled. "I fear you must deal with me, for I did not give your note—"

"Ah, my young cousin," he said, turning to face her, a smile upon his handsome countenance, "so glad you could—" He stopped short, anger narrowing his brown eyes. "What the devil?"

"Mr. Montgomery!" Gemma said, no less surprised to see the gentleman than he was to see her. "What are you doing here?"

She had only just voiced the question when she noticed how oddly Nevil held his right arm. It was bent across his chest, his hand partially concealed inside the cloak. It was not concealed quite well enough, however, for she could see his wrist and the polished metal grip of a small pocket pistol.

Gemma looked from the weapon back to Nevil's cold, passionless eyes, and in that one instant, she realized the enormity of the error she had made in suspecting Duncan of being behind the attempts on Ceddy's life. The villain was Nevil, Sir Frederick's *other* nephew. It always had been.

Though never good at dissembling, Gemma tried to school her face so it would not reveal her dawning knowledge. Unfortunately, Nevil was not deceived. He knew she had seen the weapon, and he knew as well that she understood the purpose for which he had brought it.

"So," he said, slowly raising his arm so the pistol was

pointed directly at her forehead. "Where is the boy? Speak up, for I grow weary of this game of cat-and-mouse."

Gemma tried to ignore the cold fear that crept into her bones, fear for herself as well as for the boy who was as dear to her as any brother could be.

"Your inheritance is safe," she said. "Your concern is misplaced, for Ceddy is no threat to you. Nora has refused to allow the adoption, and she has renounced any claim Ceddy may have to being Sir Frederick's heir. So you see, the boy can do you no harm."

Nevil appeared much struck by this information, though there was no lessening of the coldness in his eyes. "This is the truth?"

"Yes. Nora wrote to Lady Montgomery this afternoon asking everyone to join us at the cottage tomorrow. It was her intention to make the announcement at that time."

For several moments, Nevil appeared lost in thought, though the hand holding the pistol never wavered. "This is good news, indeed," he said. "Good for me and good for the boy. Now he can live to a ripe old age, if that is his wish." He looked at her, his face bland. " 'Tis a pity the same cannot be said for you, Miss Westin."

"Wh-what do you mean?"

"My dear young lady, you must see that I cannot allow you to return to the cottage. Now that you know my little secret, I fear there is only one way to guarantee that you never divulge it."

Gemma watched in horror as Nevil put his thumb upon the hammer of the pistol and eased it back. With his finger already beginning to squeeze the trigger, she did not waste time weighing the probabilities of his missing his target; instead, she acted purely on instinct, grabbing Nevil's wrist with both her hands and pushing it aside. Their struggle lasted no more than ten seconds, but when Nevil yanked his arm free of her grasp, slinging her to the ground, the weapon discharged and the single bullet was fired into the air.

"Fool!" he shouted, his face contorted with rage. "Do you think I cannot kill you with my bare hands?"

Not waiting for her answer, he caught hold of the front of her rubberized coat and yanked her up. Immediately he grasped her around the neck and began to squeeze, his thumbs pushing cruelly into her throat and cutting off her air supply,

Gemma could not breathe. Her ears began to ring, and an unbelievable pain started to pound inside her head. She knew she had but a few seconds left to live, and the terror and desperation she felt gave her a strength she did not know she possessed. Knowing only that she must fight back, she lifted her right leg and brought her foot down with all her might upon Nevil's toes.

Instantly he screamed and let her go, grabbing his foot in his hands and crying out in pain.

The wooden pattens Gemma wore had sliced right through the fine, soft leather of Nevil's boots, and blood already showed red between the cuts; however, Gemma did not deceive herself into believing the injury would detain the villain for long. Realizing that this was possibly her last chance for escape, she turned and ran as fast as the heavy coat and wet ground would allow. Unfortunately, the only route open to her was across the weir.

"Mind you don't stand on it," Amos had said. His words halted her just before she took the first step onto the water-logged structure.

"You'll pay for this," Nevil yelled, straightening and walking slowly toward her. "No more quick death for you. Now I mean to make it slow and painful."

Gemma looked at the crazed man who was but a few feet away from her and knew she would take her chances with the weir. After all, she had been crossing it since she was a girl. All she need do was go slowly. Hold to the hand rail. And do nothing foolish.

The first few steps were not too bad, except for the fact that fear made her knees as wobbly as India rubber, and the muddy river water that rushed over her feet rendered the wood surface as tractionless as glass. Still, she continued, inching slowly, cautiously toward the far bank.

She was halfway across to the other side when Nevil stepped onto the weir. He moved recklessly, not even bothering to use the hand rail, and though Gemma hurried her measured pace, he was soon within arm's reach of her.

Moving quickly, he took one more step and grabbed the sleeve of her coat, yanking her toward him.

"No!" she yelled.

Her protest was lost, for at that moment, the wood shivered beneath her feet, as though giving up the uneven fight with nature. Gemma clutched at the hand rail, but it was too late. One moment the weir was there, holding back the torrent of water, and the next it just disintegrated, pitching Gemma headlong into the roiling river below.

Chapter Fourteen

After Amos had taken the letter from Lady Montgomery, promising to put it into Mrs. Nora Westin's hands, Duncan turned to retrace his steps to the manor house. As it transpired, he got no farther than the end of the flagstone footpath. Because he wanted a little privacy in which to think through what he might have done or said to warrant being denied the hospitality of the cottage, he paused at the mounting block. Ignoring the discomfort of the still-damp stone, he perched upon the block and gave himself up to remembering all that had passed between him and Gemma on the occasion of their last meeting.

There had been the fire in the drawing room, of course, and the equally incendiary episode in the kitchen when she had washed his hand. In both instances, however, Duncan felt certain he had done nothing for which he need be ashamed. Quite the contrary, actually, for a less scrupulous fellow might have seized the advantage and made love to Gemma. Heaven knew *he* had wanted to do so!

When a quarter hour had passed, and Duncan still could recall nothing that would justify such censure from the ladies, he decided to try his luck again. Perhaps they had reconsidered and would give him an opportunity to explain whatever misunderstanding had arisen. Certain he was doing the right thing, he returned to the front door. He had only just lifted his hand to knock when he heard someone coming from around the side of the cottage.

Pausing, he watched quietly while the person turned the corner of the house, walked past the rose arbor, then continued down the footpath, their pattens clicking on the flagstones. It was Gemma. There was no mistaking her, even though she wore a rubberized coat and had pulled the matching hat down low so that it covered a goodly portion of her face.

Puzzled as to why she should choose to go for a walk on such a dreary afternoon—and in pattens!—he decided to follow her. Too much had happened during the past fortnight for him to feel comfortable allowing her to venture out alone, so he waited until she had crossed the lane and passed the scrub, then he followed suit, trailing her much as he had done the first day he arrived.

The journey was not easy, and Duncan decided that when he finally did catch up with Gemma, he would give her a piece of his mind for leading him such a soggy chase. Never again, he decided, would he come into East Anglia without a pair of stout boots.

Trudging along as best he could, he saw her pause beside the large hawthorn bush where he had stood that first day, concealed from view. On that particular day she had stepped up onto the weir to beckon to Ceddy to come to her, but not before she had lifted her skirt up over her shoulders and given Duncan a most provocative view of her shapely derriere. A smile pulled at the corners of his mouth as he recalled the incident. Come to think of it, he never had asked her why she had done such an odd thing. Perhaps he would—

A sudden, sharp sound rent the air; one that sent a tremor of fear coursing through Duncan's body. The sound was the unmistakable report of a handgun, and adding to Duncan's fright was the fact that he could no longer see Gemma!

He attempted to run, but the harder he tried, the more the soggy earth sucked at his boots, making every step a strength-sapping effort. While the ground slowed him to little better than a walk, his heart raced double time, jumping into his throat and threatening to choke him.

"Gemma!" he yelled. "Damnation! Where are you? Answer me."

He doubted she could hear him above the roar of the river, for aside from that one gunshot, he had heard nothing else. Still, he continued to call her name.

After what seemed an eternity, when Duncan finally reached the hawthorn bush, he stopped dead in his tracks, for the sight before him was enough to strike fear into any man's heart. Gemma was halfway across the weir, and a man in a dark, enveloping cloak was pursuing her. Duncan ceased to breathe, for the man obviously meant to climb upon the weir as well, totally disregarding the flood waters that had already reached the top of the wooden structure.

"No!" Duncan yelled. "It will not hold you both!"

The man either did not hear the warning, or he did not care. Probably the latter, for he appeared maniacal in his desire to catch Gemma, running across the water-logged boards as though nature on the rampage offered no threat to him.

As for Duncan, who watched helplessly from the shore, he felt enough terror for both of them, and when the man grabbed at Gemma, yanking her toward him, Duncan thought surely his chest would explode from the pressure of his fear. But it was not his chest that burst into a thousand pieces, it was the weir.

Everything happened at once. Almost within the same instant, the weir blew apart, Gemma and the cloaked man were pitched like hapless rag dolls into the roiling river below, and the water that had been partially subdued by the weir came gushing down upon them in a powerful wave perhaps ten feet tall.

"Gemmaaa!"

Moving as fast as humanly possible, Duncan made his way to the site where the weir had once been. In the water just below him, he spied the man whose greed and jealousy had caused this tragedy. The villain's cloak had become entangled with the roots of a beech tree that had been partially eroded by the rains, and he was being tossed endlessly back and forth in the churning water. His once-handsome face was waxen, devoid of all expression, and his lifeless form bobbed up and down like a fisherman's cork at the end of a line.

Duncan spared not even a moment's regret for Nevil Montgomery. There might be time for that later; for now, his only concern was Gemma.

At first he could not find her, and his heart nearly ceased to beat, so frightened was he that she had met a similar fate as his cousin. In the next second, however, he saw her. She had caught hold of a willow tree limb that trailed in the river, and she was hanging on to the fragile greenery with all her strength. Unfortunately, she was hampered by the rubberized coat she still wore, and she was fighting a losing battle against the rushing water.

Almost as soon as Duncan saw her, the limb broke under the strain of Gemma's weight, and she was swept downstream. Duncan did not stop to think; he merely reacted to the dictates of his heart. After stripping off his own coat, he jumped feet first into the river.

The shock of the cold, muddy torrent made him gasp, but after a couple of deep breaths, he began to swim toward the place he had last seen Gemma—if the action could be called swimming. In truth, the force of the water pretty much did with him what it wished, but at least his strong strokes kept him from being pulled under.

For what seemed like hours, but was probably no more than a matter of minutes, he was swept along by the current. Of Gemma, there was no sign, and Duncan's only piece of good luck was a chance—and for his forehead, a very painful—meeting with what he assumed was Ceddy's boat dock, or what was left of it.

Grateful for any help, no matter how dearly paid for, Duncan ignored his aching head and clung to the wood planks. When the river began to broaden and the current slowed down somewhat, he managed to pull himself aboard the dock for a much needed respite.

Once he was out of the water, he looked all around him for any sign of Gemma. Just when he despaired of ever seeing her again, he spotted her not twenty feet ahead of him, still encased in the rubberized coat. Miraculously, she was still alive. She, too, had found a piece of lifesaving debris, one that looked like it might have been part of the weir. Whatever it was, her arms were wrapped around it, and she clung to it tenaciously, like a stubborn, indomitable limpet.

"Gemma! Over here!"

Somehow she heard him, for she turned her head, her eyes frantically seeking a glimpse of him. When her search was rewarded, the expression on her face showed a blend of surprise, relief, and wonder. Duncan knew just how she felt, for that same wonder was coursing through him.

"Gemma!" he called again.

"Duncan!" she yelled, letting go her piece of debris just long enough to wave her arm to him. "Oh, Duncan. I cannot believe that you found me."

Within seconds he was in the water again, holding on to the dock with one arm and swimming toward Gemma with the other. Then, as if in answer to his prayers, he was beside her, reaching out his hand to her, clasping her firmly by the wrist and pulling her to him. Wasting no time, he boosted her up onto the piece of dock, then climbed up beside her. For the remainder of their watery journey, they lay locked in each other's arms.

How they finally came to rest, they were never able to say. All they knew for certain was that the torrent finally subsided, and their makeshift raft drifted into a hodge-podge of debris that had piled against a little spit of land jutting out from the riverbank. Using their last bits of strength, Duncan and Gemma slogged through the hip-deep water until they reached the shore, where they collapsed upon the beautiful, glorious, wonderful, soggy ground, too tired to go any farther.

When Gemma began to cry softly, Duncan put his arm around her waist and drew her close, so that her back was solidly against his chest. While he fitted his knees into the bend of her knees, he whispered words of comfort in her ear. "You are safe now, my love, my brave, wonderful girl. Do not cry, for I promise you, all will be well."

"Nev-Nevil," she managed to say, then shuddered with the effort. "He—"

"Do not think of him, my sweet. Nevil will never hurt anyone again."

Gemma sighed, giving herself up to the assurance of Duncan's words and the marvelous feeling of his arm around her, holding her close. Very soon she heard his slow, rhythmic breathing and knew that he slept.

She remained awake a full minute longer, reveling in being alive and in the arms of the man she loved—the man who was innocent of any wrongdoing. After sparing a moment to offer a prayer of thanksgiving, she snuggled as close to Duncan as was humanly possible and let deep, healing sleep claim her as well.

Morning sunlight woke her. Or perhaps it was the sound of approaching horses. Whatever the cause, Gemma came awake with a start. "Easy," Duncan said, gently brushing a lock of hair back from her forehead. "You are safe."

They had not moved from the spot where they collapsed last evening, but they were no longer fitted together like two spoons. Now Gemma lay on her back. At some time during the night her one remaining boot had been removed, that and the rubberized coat, which had been pulled up over her like a blanket.

As for Duncan, he was stretched out beside her, but propped on his left elbow where he could look his fill of her face. It was a task to which he gave his full attention. "Did I ever tell you," he said softly, tracing the tip of his finger across the bridge of her nose and over her cheekbone, "how much I like those freckles?"

"No," she replied a bit breathlessly, "I do not believe you did."

He let his finger travel to her temple and around the curve of her ear, then he pressed his palm against the side of her face. "And your eyes," he said. "Did I happen to mention how a man could look into those blue orbs for an eternity and never miss the sky?"

Gemma could find nothing to dislike in this particular form of early-morning conversation. As for the feel of Duncan's slightly rough palm against her skin, that she liked even better than the words. "Odd," she said, gazing up at him, "that you should like blue, for I have discovered in myself a fondness for green eyes. Green with little flecks of gold near the centers."

She could have looked at him all day, though a deep gash bisected his forehead and his cheeks were covered with morning stubble. Reaching up, she touched his face, and at the contact, his green eyes darkened, unmistakable passion making the pupils appear almost black. "Gemma—"

"Jamison!" someone yelled. "Miss Westin! Can you hear me?"

Gemma had not imagined the sound of horses, for now they were quite close. Horses and men.

"Jamison! Are you there?"

"Steven!" Duncan called out in answer. "We are here."

Duncan sat up, then he rose to his feet, but not without some difficulty. When Gemma would have followed his example, her entire body protested. "Ohh," she moaned.

"Do not try to move," he said.

She was obliged to take his advice, for every bone felt battered, every muscle was stiff, and dull pain throbbed from the top of her head down to her toes.

"Remain where you are," Duncan continued. "That voice you heard belongs to my friend, Steven Yarborough, and unless my ears deceive me, he has brought a farm wagon to convey us home. Though how he managed to find us so quickly, I cannot even imagine.''

"Amos Littlejohn," Gemma said without needing to give the matter any great thought. "Depend upon it, Amos will have shown your friend the way.''

Chapter Fifteen

" 'I am come into deep waters,' " Mr. Bascombe Newley
said, his raised voice easily drifting through Gemma's bedchamber window from the wildflower garden below,
" 'where the floods overflow me.' Psalms sixty-nine, two."

"As you say," an older and far more restrained voice
said. "But I should rather quote an earlier psalm, Mr.
Newley, one more in keeping with what *is*, rather than
what *was*. 'This is the day the Lord hath made; we will
rejoice and be glad in it.' "

"Of course, sir," the curate added. "Psalms sixty-six,
verse twenty-four." From the sound of it, Mr. Newley was
not best pleased to have the tables turned on him, obviously
deeming Scripture-quoting as his own personal province,
even if the other quoter was a gentleman as worthy of
respect as Sir Frederick Montgomery.

Gemma had suspected that the purpose of the younger
gentleman's visit was a private interview with her, so the
instant she saw the curate's ancient whiskey stop in the
lane beside the mounting block, she had fled. Abandoning

with regret the sun-drenched bench beneath the rose arbor, where she had been conversing with Sir Frederick and letting the healing warmth of the sun perform its magic upon her sore muscles, Gemma had sought the privacy of her bedchamber.

When Mr. Newley realized he was to be denied his objective, he chose to remain at Howarth Cottage for only a few minutes, using the exigencies of the Sabbath as his excuse for leaving. "Please inform Miss Gemma that I shall give myself the pleasure of calling upon her again some time tomorrow."

While Nora was abovestairs in Gemma's bedchamber delivering the curate's message, another gentleman arrived, one whose coming was greeted with far more enthusiasm than was shown the previous caller.

"Steven, my boy," Sir Frederick said, "what a pleasure to see you."

"And you, Sir Frederick."

From the warm exchange of greetings, Gemma concluded that the two gentlemen were friends of some duration. As for the degree of friendship existing between the newcomer and her stepmother, the sudden blush that came to Nora's cheeks told Gemma all she needed to know upon that subject.

"I regret having missed you yesterday afternoon," the elderly gentleman said. "I called at the cottage to offer what comfort I might to Nora, and you may imagine my happiness when I discovered Duncan sitting in the parlor, battered and bruised, but very much alive."

While the Westin ladies sat on the edge of Gemma's bed, eavesdropping unashamedly, Sir Frederick paused to regain control of his emotions. "Nora informed me," he said finally, "that you had only just carried the young lady up to her bedchamber, then ridden off for the apothecary. Under the circumstances, I thought the best thing I could do for the ladies was to refrain from getting under foot, so I left almost immediately. Now, however, I hope you will allow me to extend my heartfelt appreciation to you for rescuing Jamison and Miss Westin."

"I assure you, sir, there was no rescuing needed, for they had come through the worst of it all on their own. As for locating them, I can take no credit for that, either. Any praise is to be laid at the servant's door. I merely followed Littlejohn's lead. He is a very handy fellow to have around."

"Yes, so I have been told. An uncanny chap that, and I mean to see he is properly rewarded."

An uncomfortable silence fell, and Sir Frederick cleared his throat. "Amos was instrumental in retrieving from the river the body of my other nephew, Mr. Nevil Montgomery. Following the coroner's inquest tomorrow morning, Nevil will be conveyed to his home for burial."

The elderly gentleman cleared his throat again. "A sorry mess, this. I should have taken better precautions so no one would discover my plans for Ceddy until the business was settled. Servants hear more than we realize, and they often reveal things they should not. But who could have foretold such instability on Nevil's part?"

"Who, indeed?"

There was silence again, then Mr. Steven Yarborough asked, ever so casually, if the planned journey to Chelmsford had been canceled.

"Canceled? By no means. As soon as Miss Westin feels up to traveling, Lady Montgomery and I intend to whisk the three of them off to Montgomery Park with all haste."

"Will their stay be long, do you think, sir?"

"If I have anything to say to the matter, it will be permanent."

"Well, now," Mr. Yarborough said, his manner noticeably more relaxed, "that is good news. I had been searching my brain for some reasonable sounding excuse to get Nora—Mrs. Westin, that is—to the area.''

After a quick intake of breath, Nora sat still as a stone. Her eyes were closed and her fingers were laced so tightly they had begun to turn white, and if anyone had asked Gemma, she would have told them she doubted the lady breathed again for a full minute.

"And what is it to you," Sir Frederick asked, suspicion in his tone, "where Mrs. Westin does or does not go?"

"I wish to show her Yarborough Grange."

Nora caught her bottom lip between her teeth to stop its trembling.

"I realize, sir, that the grange is nothing like as fine an estate as Montgomery Park, nor even Howarth Manor, but it is a pretty place, and quite comfortable, and I believe Nora will not find it contemptible. Furthermore, the property brings in a respectable income, and there is plenty of room for Ceddy and any brothers and sisters."

"Why, you impudent young dog! Lady Montgomery and I only just got the lad and his mother back into our lives, and here you are trying to steal them from us. I believe I shall have to call you out."

Mr. Yarborough chuckled. "I beg you to reconsider that scheme, sir. After all, the grange is situated but four miles from Montgomery Park. Such a distance is negligible, assuring almost daily visits between the families. That is, if my Lorelei accepts the offer of my hand."

"What did you call her?"

"Mrs. Westin," he corrected. "A slip of the tongue. Pray, do not regard it."

If the lady was displeased by that slip of the tongue, she gave no evidence of her displeasure. Her eyes were open at last, and no one viewing the brilliance of their shine, or the smile that would not be denied her lips, could be in any doubt as to the answer she would give the brawny Mr. Yarborough when he finally put his luck to the test.

For a full hour after Nora left the bedchamber, Gemma pondered all she had overheard. Never had it occurred to her that a woman thirty-four years old, and twice widowed, might marry again. Not that Gemma did not wish every happiness for Nora; she loved her too much to begrudge her a full life with a home and a loving husband. Still, she could not help wondering what her own situation might be once Nora remarried.

Of course, Gemma knew what she would like it to be. She wanted to spend the rest of her life with Duncan Jamison. In his arms. By his side. His wife, his lover, his friend.

"Gemma," Ceddy said, tapping at the door, then entering even before he was invited to do so. His young boy's face was alight with excitement and curiosity. "A gift has just arrived for you."

"A gift? What sort of gift?"

"This sort."

Ceddy brought from behind his back a medium-sized box, beautifully wrapped and adorned with a large green bow.

Gemma could not imagine who would be sending her such a package, and while she stared, trying to guess the identity of the sender, Ceddy said, "There is a card as well." He extended the white pasteboard while still retaining the gift.

Gemma's hands trembled as she read the bold handwriting.

> *To the bravest lady I know.*
> *Will you accept another challenge?*

*If so, don the enclosed and meet
me on the other side of the scrub.
Yours, etc.
D. Jamison, Esquire*

Silently she held out her hand for the box, then she set it on her lap. It was the work of a moment to untie the green bow and unfold the pretty, handpainted paper. Inside, concealed in layers of fragile tissue paper, was a pair of intricately carved pattens.

Ceddy's excitement evaporated like breath exhaled on a winter's day. "Pattens? What a hum! I vow I was never so taken in. Who would give such a dull, boring gift?"

If the lad was disappointed by the mundane footwear, not so the young lady, for she held them to her heart, a smile on her face. "I can find nothing to dislike. If the truth be known, I consider them quite imaginative."

"But you detest having to wear pattens," Ceddy insisted.

"Not these," she said. "I wished on a star last night, and if my wish has come true, I may never want to take these off."

Muttering something about females having bats in their belfries, Ceddy took himself off, leaving Gemma free to run to her clothes press to find the lavender-blue frock Duncan had admired once before. After straightening the square neckline, then pinching her cheeks to give them a little added color, she hurried down the stairs and out the entrance door.

As before, the pattens clicked upon the flagstone pathway, but this time the sound was like music to Gemma's ears. This time she went not to meet a coward who hid behind anonymous notes, but the man she loved. Duncan Jamison had issued her a mysterious challenge, and though she dared not let herself dwell overlong on the nature of that challenge, it was enough that she was to see him.

Thankfully, no one saw her leave the cottage, so she continued unimpeded to the lane and beyond. Two days of sunshine had done much to disperse the puddles in the lane, but Gemma was obliged to use caution when traversing the springy ground to the scrub.

"You came," Duncan said, stepping out in the open to meet her. He wore his bottle-green coat and fawn breeches, and on his forehead, a court plaster covered the cut he had sustained while in the river. If in the whole of England there was a handsomer man, Gemma took leave to doubt it.

"Of course I came," she said, then she lifted one foot to reveal the pattens strapped to her boots. "How could I refuse? With a gift to bribe me and a challenge to intrigue me, I had no choice. Especially not when the giver of both the gift and the challenge was the same man who jumped into a raging river to save me."

"You saved yourself," he said. "I just went along for the ride."

"You were very brave to do so, sir."

"And you, madam, were just plain brave." His voice was suddenly husky. "When I saw the weir disintegrate and pitch you into the air, I feared my entire world was about to come to an end."

"Please," she said, her own voice none too steady, "do not say such things unless you mean them."

He took her hands in his and urged her toward him. "I never meant anything more. If I could gaze no more into your blue eyes, I should never wish to look upon the sky again. Without the gold of your hair, I should be obliged to shun the sun. And without your courage, your spirit, the world would lose its savor, and I should never again find joy."

While he spoke, he drew her closer and closer until their bodies touched, then he placed her arms around his waist and took her face in his hands. With soft, gentle kisses, one after another, he worked his way from her cheekbone, across her pert nose, and to the other cheekbone. "My sweet Gemma," he said, "the angels were there before me, but now all the kisses on your lovely face were placed there by me."

"For the first time in my life, I wish I had more freckles."

Understanding her perfectly, Duncan chuckled, then he bent and brushed his lips against the side of her neck. "Would you like one there?" he asked.

"Oh, yes. Most definitely there."

"And what of this area here?" he asked, letting his mouth linger in the hollow of her throat.

Gemma thought her heart would leap right out of her chest, it beat so hard. "That spot must never again be without a freckle."

"And here?" he said, working his way up her neck to the pulse that throbbed behind her ear.

"Oh, my, yes. If the truth be known, I think I feel the tiniest little freckle materializing behind my other ear."

"Here?" he asked. When he touched the pulse there with the tip of his tongue, Gemma grew so warm she wondered if it was possible to incinerate in one's own body heat.

Unable to stop herself, she turned her face up to his, offering him her lips. "Do you see anything here?" she asked.

She heard the sharp intake of his breath before he bent and claimed her lips, kissing her until she thought she might faint from the magic of his touch.

The bones that once supported her knees seemed to melt in the warmth of his embrace, and Gemma was forced to lean against him or fall.

When she pressed against him, she heard him moan, then a moment later his hands were on her shoulders and he was easing her away. "While I can still speak," he said, "perhaps I should issue that challenge."

"Challenge?" she said, far too interested in renewing that freckle search to care about anything else. "Must we play games?"

"I believe you might like the one I have in mind," he said, "for I wonder if you dare become a politician's wife?"

For a moment, Gemma was not certain she had heard him correctly. "Wife? You want me to marry you?"

"Yes, my beautiful girl, for I do not think I can live without you. I love you, and I want to be with you now and through eternity."

A moment ago, when Duncan's kisses were setting her on fire, Gemma thought she had never been so happy in her entire life. Now, of course, Duncan had said he loved her, and she realized that her happiness had only just begun.

"Well, my sweet, what is it to be? Do you love me?"

"Oh, yes. I love you with all my heart."

"Then will you be my wife and let me love you forever? Will you accept the challenge?"

"Yes," she said, easing her way back into his arms. "I accept."

ABOUT THE AUTHOR

Martha Kirkland lives with her family in Atlanta, Georgia. She is the author of three Zebra regency romances: *The Gallant Gambler*, *Three For Brighton*, and *The Noble Nephew*. Martha is currently working on her next Zebra regency romance, *The Seductive Spy*, which will be published in March 1999. Martha loves to hear from her readers and you may write to her c/o Zebra Books. Please include a self-addressed stamped envelope if you wish a response. Or you may e-mail her at talkirkland@mindspring.com.

BOOK YOUR PLACE ON OUR WEBSITE AND MAKE THE READING CONNECTION!

We've created a customized website just for our very special readers, where you can get the inside scoop on everything that's going on with Zebra, Pinnacle and Kensington books.

When you come online, you'll have the exciting opportunity to:

- View covers of upcoming books
- Read sample chapters
- Learn about our future publishing schedule (listed by publication month *and author*)
- Find out when your favorite authors will be visiting a city near you
- Search for and order backlist books from our online catalog
- Check out author bios and background information
- Send e-mail to your favorite authors
- Meet the Kensington staff online
- Join us in weekly chats with authors, readers and other guests
- Get writing guidelines
- AND MUCH MORE!

Visit our website at
http://www.zebrabooks.com

WATCH FOR THESE ZEBRA REGENCIES

WATCH FOR THESE REGENCY ROMANCES